BOUND

THE MYSTERY OF LANDON MILLER BOOK TWO

R. M. GAUTHIER

Printed in the United States of America

First Printing, 2017

Starlight Publishing

17 Flamingo Crescent

North York, ON

M6M4E9

www.rmgauthier.com

ISBN-13: 978-0-9949489-4-6

CONTENTS

CHAPTER 1

*a*s I sit here, my leg bouncing up and down uncontrollably with my hands glued to the armrests on either side of me, I'm freaking out. Panic washes over me, taking complete control of my body leaving me more than anxious. My mind drifts to the circumstances that have brought me to my current situation.

Weeks of investigation.

Weeks of worried concern.

Weeks of having everyone refuse to cooperate with me, or give me any information. The knowledge I discovered, I found on my own. But, finding the truth can be difficult when you're left in the dark.

Leroy insisted it was for my own safety.

Agent Johnson tried to contain me.

However, nothing on this planet, or universe, can stop me from uncovering what happened that horrendous night in my living room. The world, as I discovered, is not a pleasant place. There were so many things I wasn't aware of, even more I wish I hadn't figured out. But, now I realize this knowledge is necessary and I will go to any lengths, fight anyone, in order to return my life to normal again.

Which brings me to the reason I'm sitting on a plane, my fingers turning white from squeezing the armrest too hard. I don't like flying. Scratch that, I hate flying, but as I've stated, wild horses can't keep me from achieving my goal.

The captain's voice startles me from my thoughts.

"We are making our descent, please remain in your seats with your seatbelts fastened until the plane has come to a complete stop. It has been a pleasure having you travel with us. Have a safe journey and we hope to see you soon."

Now it's time for the worst part of flying––the landing. Landing is something I hate most. If something goes wrong, chances are it will be during the landing.

I remain in my seat as directed, my knuckles turning white from clenching my hands so tight. I squeeze my eyes shut while waiting to live or die. At this point, it's unclear which choice is better.

"Hey. Are you all right?" His soft voice breaks through my panicked state as a warm hand covers mine.

"No," I answer while clenching my teeth. "But I will be once we're safely on the ground."

"We are on the ground. We're fine. You can open your eyes now," he replies as if he's talking to a child.

Or perhaps, that's how one speaks to a person standing on a ledge ready to jump. Either way, it sounds condescending and I'm annoyed. However, I open my eyes.

Gazing back at me are two huge blue eyes full of worry, which belong to the one person who offered help through this entire ordeal.

"Are you sure you're okay?" he repeats, unsure of my response.

"Yes, I'm fine. Are we really on the ground?"

"Yeah. We've made it," he replies, scrutinizing me as if I may break down at any moment.

I shake my head, reassuring my stability.

He smiles a little before speaking again. "In that case." He looks down at my hand. "Might I have my arm back...?" He looks up at me, then back at my hand. "Please," he begs, obviously holding in the pain.

Following his line of sight down to my hand, shock courses through me. I'm a little more than horrified to see it's not the armrest I am squeezing too hard, but rather his arm. I pull my hand away, mumbling an embarrassed apology.

"Sorry," I whisper, looking back at his face.

He's wearing an amused expression while he pulls his arm away, rubbing the area my hand held in a death grip not moments ago.

"It's okay. We're here, everything is fine. Let's get off this plane and get to where we need to be." He stands up and grabs our bags from the overhead compartment.

I stand, stretching a little, before picking up my bag from the seat where he deposited it and throwing it over my shoulder. We follow the rest of the crowd off the plane and into the airport.

Once inside we follow the signs that lead us to our car

rental booth. He proceeds to the counter to deal with our reservation, while I sit with our bags.

We're here and I'm finally going to put an end to this nightmare.

Once he finishes at the counter we make our way out of the airport to the parking facility. We find our rental, place our bags in the trunk and situate ourselves in the vehicle.

"I got one with a GPS, so we'll know where we're going," he offers.

"Good idea, because I'm not sure, even if we asked for directions, we would understand them anyway." I laugh.

"Well, I do know some Italian, but not enough to get us anywhere." He smiles, as he pulls out of the parking garage.

We are finally underway and getting closer to where I need to be. Closer to where my world exists. Closer to my heart.

"It's going to be about an hour and a half. So, get comfortable," he declares.

"Yeah, I know. I've studied enough about this place." Turning, I watch out the passenger window, while he drives through the city.

Once we reach the outskirts of the city, there is a vast amount of empty space. From my own research, I know there's not much to see on the way, but I don't care. This is not a vacation. We're not here to admire the views. Maybe someday I'll return for some sightseeing, but for today, I'm on a mission and will stop at nothing to get what I came for.

Those thoughts lead me back to that night so many weeks ago. The night my world turned upside down. As my eyes drift through the vast emptiness of land spread out in front of me, my mind wanders to thoughts of that night, which has been cemented in my memory.

As the memories come rushing back I close my eyes I can see what happened replaying in my mind.

CHAPTER 2

*W*hat the hell just happened? I open my eyes quickly just to make sure it really happened. I drop onto the couch as my world comes crashing down around me. My chest tightens, the pressure excruciating like someone's squeezing it between their hands.

Did that just happen? Did, Landon Miller, really just walk out of my house with his Master?

Master?

That strange, frightening man, Alistair, is Landon's Master?

How can this be?

And, what's with the tattoo or branding?

Landon's branded?

Completely unaware of what is happening, two arms circle around me and I'm being pulled into someone's chest. I barely hear what Haley's saying as she's wiping my cheeks with her finger tips and I wonder why.

Reaching up I feel wetness. Tears are streaming down my face.

When did I start crying?

"Lexi?" Haley speaks softly.

I pull back from her hug and gaze at her face.

"Lexi?" she repeats.

"What?" I snap, inadvertently.

"Are you? Shit. Of course, you're not okay. Jesus, what happened?" Haley's questions tumble from her lips, displaying her bewilderment. I share the sentiment.

Haley sits back on the couch deep in thought, confusion written all over her face. After a moment of hesitation, she turns to me.

"Well one thing is for certain, I'm going to get to the bottom of this." She hugs me once more, then rises from the couch.

"What the hell was that?" she yells unexpectedly to no one in particular.

In the quiet room her voice carries, causing me to jump.

Leroy scowls at her but remains silent.

I glance around the room and notice three other men have appeared in my living room. I recognize one of them as a bartender from Landon's club. The other two I've not seen before. All three have cell phones pressed to their ears, but turn and glare at Haley after her outburst.

Not a word is uttered as the room goes completely silent.

"I asked a question and would appreciate an answer." Haley looks deliberately at each man. "Now!" she emphasizes.

I shudder at her tone.

No one moves.

No one makes a sound.

Everyone gawks at Haley as if she's a wild animal ready to pounce, which is probably true.

Finally, Leroy steps forward holding his hands up in surrender.

"Miss Rose, please calm down."

"Calm down. Really, that's what you have to say to me. I'll tell you what, I'll calm down once you explain to me exactly what went on here tonight. Okay?"

I stand up from the couch, moving to her side.

"Leroy? Please. Tell me what that was?" I point to the floor where only a short while ago Landon was kneeling.

"Ms. Waters." Leroy looks me dead in the eye trying to relay something. The fact he used my maiden name should tell me something, but it's not registering. I want answers and if there's an absence of explanation, there's no telling what I might do.

"Cut the crap, Leroy. My name is Lexi," I hiss at him, malice thick in my words. "I want to know what's happened here and I want to know now."

"I'm sorry Lexi, it's not my place to tell you." He drops his gaze to the floor refusing to look me in the eye. "He wouldn't want me to tell you." His eyes meet mine as he pleads with me to understand.

"Well, somebody better start talking," Haley barks, anger clear in her tone and on her face as she scrutinizes everyone in the room. "Now."

"Look, we're handling things. We're all working to help

Landon. So please. Calm down and have a seat." Leroy tries to use his authority to control the situation.

Clearly, his attempt is not working as my mind screams. *Calm down? Have a seat? That's his answer?* Well, that's not going to fly with me. This is my house. He has no authority here.

Immediately I head to the front hall, scoop up my purse and start digging through it. I find my cell phone and frantically begin pushing the screen because the number I want right now is saved in my contacts. I don't know why I saved it, but I'm sure glad I did.

If Leroy won't offer his assistance, I knew somebody who might.

The entire room watches me as if I'm about to pull out a Beretta and start shooting the place up. I press the green call button, and the phone begins dialing before pressing it to my ear. It rings twice before it's answered.

"Hey, it's Mrs. Shaw. I need your help." I speak calmly into the phone.

"I'm on my way," he confirms, then the line goes dead.

I hang up, move back to the couch and resume my position to wait. Haley sits beside me waiting for an explanation that will never come.

"Lexi? Who did you call?" she whispers.

"Somebody I'm hoping can help, or at the very least give us some answers." My gaze locks on Leroy.

The words are for him.

He watches me as he continues his call.

Relaxing back on the couch, my mind is in a frenzy thinking about everything that's happened. It's hard to believe it's only been a month since I sat on this couch, bored and determined to change my life. Well, mission accomplished, my life has certainly changed. Now I wonder if it was for better or worse. While deliberating my existence in the world, the front door bursts open and Agent Johnson strolls in.

"What's happened?" he asks, loud and clear.

"What are you doing here?" Leroy scoffs at him.

"Mrs. Shaw called me. Now, tell me what's happening."

"Agent Johnson." I jump up and walk over to him, relieved help has arrived.

"Mrs. Shaw? Are you okay?" He bypasses Leroy on his way to me.

"Yes, I'm fine. It's not me. It's Landon."

"Landon?" His face scrunches and eyebrows furrow.

"Lexi." Leroy throws a warning in my direction.

I ignore him, my attention fully on Agent Johnson.

"Tell me, Lexi. I can help him," he whispers to me.

"They took him," I cry out.

Agent Johnson wraps his arms around me allowing me a moment of sobbing like a child. Once I'm in full control of my faculties again, I resume my explanation.

"He came into my house. Threatened all of us. Then, he took Landon with him," I babble, incoherently.

"Who Lexi? Tell me who took Landon?" He grips both of my shoulders to keep me from collapsing.

"That guy in the pictures you showed me."

I hear a loud gasp from behind Agent Johnson.

"What pictures?" Leroy's angry voice slices through the room making me shudder. When no one speaks, he tries again. "Lexi, what pictures are you talking about?" He strides over to stand next to Agent Johnson.

I take a step back glancing between them. I have no idea what to do or tell them. I'm way out of my element here and don't know who to trust. All I know is Landon is in trouble and he needs my help. The only way I know how to help him is to involve Agent Johnson. He is, after all, an FBI agent who has resources not available to us.

"Which guy, Alexandria?" Agent Johnson asks breathlessly.

"The strange looking one. The one with the dark hair?"

Agent Johnson takes a step back, alarm evident in his features.

"Damn it." He turns around, pulls out his cell phone and stabs it furiously with his forefinger.

"What pictures, Alexandria?" Leroy's anger is evident in his tone.

I have a quick debate with myself considering my options and how much information I should reveal to Leroy. His reluctance to offer any information has me hesitant to share in return.

Taking a hasty glance around, not only are Leroy and his three henchmen here, but Agent Johnson has brought reinforcements with him as well. There are four other men in suits—clearly agents—standing in my living room. This space is beginning to feel a lot smaller with all these huge men occupying the space.

While gazing at everyone in the room it occurs to me the more information these people have the better my chances are to bring Landon home. So I turn my attention to Leroy.

"Several weeks ago Agent Johnson came to see me. He told me he was investigating Landon, Alistair, and James. At the time, I told him I didn't know any of them, but he didn't believe me. I'm a terrible liar, and when he was leaving my house, Landon had just arrived."

"What kind of investigation?" Leroy asks.

"One I would never expose," Agent Johnsons' voice interrupts as he strolls over to join us.

"Why would you be investigating Landon? You know who the criminals are," Leroy retorts.

"Do I?" Agent Johnson counters.

Great, this is just what I need—a pissing contest. This has to stop. I need their help—both of them.

"Stop it." I screech. "Focus, please. We need to help Landon and if that means we all have to work together, then so be it."

Both Agent Johnson and Leroy look at each other, sizing each other up and annoying the shit out of me. I have to put a stop to all this testosterone or we'll never get anything accomplished.

"Somebody needs to start from the beginning and tell me what is really going on here." I glance between them.

"First, I cannot and will not reveal anything about my investigation to the likes of him." Agent Johnson jabs his thumb in Leroy's direction. "And second, I cannot and will not involve you."

"Ditto." Leroy adds.

"It is not up to you two what I'm involved in! What

gives either of you the right to make decisions for me?" I ask, through clenched teeth.

"Mrs. Shaw…" I cut Leroy off swiftly.

"Cut the crap Leroy, we know each other by now."

The tension in the room is thick as silence fills the space.

"Okay, enough is enough," Haley barks. "Somebody better start explaining what went on here tonight, or I won't be responsible for my actions." She glares between Leroy and Agent Johnson.

"Haley," I whisper.

"What?" She glances my way. "I've had it, Lexi. These two need to start talking." She returns her glare to them. "Now."

After a pause, Leroy spins facing Haley head on.

"Miss Rose, if you don't calm yourself, I'll have you removed from this house. Do. You. Understand?" he roars back.

My body shudders at the sound of his loud, domineering voice. I glare at him, ready to intercede if the situation escalates. A quiet unassuming voice slices through the tense standoff.

"Everyone needs to calm down." Agent Johnson says in a soft, but commanding tone, placing his hand on Leroy's arm as if he's holding him back. "Miss Rose, please have a seat," he requests while putting himself between Leroy and Haley.

I'm bewildered and paralyzed by fear, praying this won't turn into a brawl. The scene is unpredictable, like a bomb ready to explode. The silence is deafening, you can hear a pin drop as everyone stands watching each other.

Can this situation possibly get worse?

Shockingly, Haley takes a seat on the couch in a very uncharacteristic move.

"Look. Just tell us what is happening. Please." I plead to both men hoping at least one will give some kind of explanation.

The quiet in the room is broken as an obscure man in the corner steps forward and speaks to Leroy.

"Sir. We have to leave immediately." he states, urgently.

Leroy gives him a sideways glance and a nod before bringing his gaze back to me. "Lexi, I wish I could tell you." His voice trails off, facial features twisting into what appears to be regret while shifting his gaze to the floor. "But, I can't. I'm sorry," he mutters, as his eyes rise to meet mine again. "I have to go. Please, stay out of this. Please," he requests before turning to Agent Johnson. His expression turns hard and cold as he pins him with a glare.

Agent Johnson glances at me, then back to Leroy. They have a silent conversation before Agent Johnson gives Leroy a slight nod and steps out of his path.

Leroy walks toward the front door, while his men follow him.

Agent Johnson watches them leave then returns his attention to me.

"Lexi, can you tell me exactly what happened?"

I consider how much to reveal as I glance at Haley who raises an eyebrow. My gaze turns back to Agent Johnson.

"You tell me what you know, and I'll tell you what I know."

Agent Johnson takes a deep breath, eyebrows creasing in frustration. "This is not a game we're playing."

"Don't you think I know that? Landon is in trouble. Are you going to tell me what I need to know or not?" I move to stand toe to toe with the agent.

"Not." He holds my glare.

It's a battle I'm ready for. I walk around him snatching my purse off the end table. I dig through it until I find the card I'm looking for. I can hear Agent Johnson attempting to interrogate Haley and almost burst out laughing as she responds.

"Do you know who you are talking to?" Her voice raises a couple of octaves.

Picking up the telephone, I dial the number on the card. While I wait for an answer, my attention returns to my best friend as she boomerangs Agent Johnson's interrogation back at him. Their behavior would be amusing if my annoyance level wasn't so high. Ignoring them, I listen to the phone ring three times before it's answered by a groggy voice.

"Hello." He attempts to sound alert.

"Dr. Miller?" I ask, even though I'm one hundred percent certain it's him.

"This is he." He sounds more awake.

A silence fills the room around me as I look between Haley and Agent Johnson who are both gaping at me.

"It's Alexandria Shaw."

"Lexi? What's wrong? Are you okay?" he inquires quickly, no doubt thinking the worst case scenarios.

"I'm fine. I'm okay. It's not me," I pause, immediately regretting this phone call. I didn't think about having to deliver this kind of news, but can't do anything about it now. "It's—Landon," I whisper.

There's a long pause before Dr. Miller speaks again.

"What's happened, Lexi? Did he?" He hesitates once again, and I immediately know where his thoughts have gone.

"No, I'm fine. Really," I reassure him. I take a moment and a deep breath before the floodgates open and the babbling begins. "He was here. And they—they took him." I begin sobbing uncontrollably.

Two arms circle around me as the phone is snatched from my hand.

Haley tugs me over to the couch forcing me to sit down, while Agent Johnson takes over my phone call. Between sobs, I hear Agent Johnson explaining to Dr. Miller what little information he knows. A flash of guilt washes over me listening to the one-sided conversation. It should be me describing the situation to Dr. Miller, not some cop in the middle of the night.

I compose myself enough to resume the conversation.

"May I have the phone back? Please?" I ask Agent Johnson.

He peers at me, assessing my sanity before handing the phone over.

"Dr. Miller, it's me again. I'm so sorry, but I didn't know who else to call," I whisper.

"It's fine, Lexi. I'm very glad you called. Is everyone else okay?" he asks.

"Yes, nothing happened. Except—well, they took Landon with them," I repeat.

"Can you answer one question for me, Lexi?" His voice resembles someone talking to a small child.

"Anything."

"Did Landon?" He clears his throat. "Did he go willingly?"

"It would appear so." My voice reveals all my pain, as memories of Landon walking out of here flash through my mind.

Dr. Miller's voice pulls me from my thoughts.

"I want you to listen to me, Lexi." His tone commanding, similar to Landon's.

"Okay."

"Stay with Agent Johnson, make certain he doesn't leave you alone. Can you do that for me?" he requests sounding parental.

"What is going on, Dr. Miller?" My anxiety is through the roof.

"Just do what I have asked, Alexandria. Please." The line goes silent.

I listen to the dial tone for a second before putting the phone back in its holder. I stumble back to the couch, placing my elbows on my knees, my head in my hands. This is bad. Really bad.

He called me Alexandria. The way he spoke was completely uncharacteristic of the Dr. Miller I met not so long ago. At that time he was pleasant, caring and soft-spoken. That man—the man on the phone—sounded more like Landon.

Can I do what he requested?

Hell no. I need to find out what is going on and since no one associated with Landon will clue me in, I guess I'm on my own.

I pull my hands from my face when Haley's voice breaks through my thoughts.

"Lexi, answer me please," she begs.

"What?" I ask, apparently having missed everything. "What did you say?" My mind returns to the here and now.

"I asked what Dr. Miller said?" she asks anxiously.

"Nothing, really," I huff. "He told me to stay with Agent Johnson. To make sure I'm not alone." My gaze falls on Agent Johnson.

He watches me for a moment as if trying to solve a puzzle, then spins away. He swiftly strides to one of his men and engages in a hushed conversation. The man leaves the house, while Agent Johnson returns to stand in front of me.

"Lexi, I'm going to leave two officers here. I want you to stay in the house. Do not leave for any reason. Understood?" he commands.

"Do I have a choice?" I whisper, as I peek up at his grim face.

"No." He marches through the living room, slamming the front door closed on his way out.

Two men, who look more like bouncers than FBI agents, remain in my living room. One stays by the hall leading to the front door. The other strolls across the room and takes a position by the hall that leads to the back door and garage, the only other way in and out of my house.

I assume they are here to protect me and are only following orders, but I'm beyond furious having my rights taken away in one swoop. I want to call everyone from the police, to SWAT teams, to the God damn National Guard to figure this all out. Sadly, there is nothing I can do except sit here and wait for word from... honestly, I have no idea who will tell anything to me.

"Lexi?" Haley says.

My attention flips back to her. She's been so quiet, I almost forgot she was here. Seeing her astonished expression reveals to me how in the dark she is. She knows even less then I do.

"Lexi. For the last time tonight, what is going on?"

"I don't know," I mutter.

"What did Landon's father say?"

"Nothing, really." Tears fill my eyes.

"That's what you said, but he must have said something?"

"No. Well, he did ask if Landon went with them willingly."

Haley sits back on the couch deep in thought.

"Why do you think he asked that?" I ask.

"I don't know." She glances around the room. "But, I'll tell you this... I won't rest until I find out." Her voice comes out in full force.

Abruptly, she stands up and marches over to the front window, peering out into the dark night.

An explanation escapes me. How much is too much? I

know there's a lot I don't know, but she is even more clueless.

"Lexi?" Her voice snaps me from my thoughts and I glance at her. "What was all the talk about photographs, an investigation?" She glides back over and sits down.

Hesitating momentarily, I feel bad that I've kept all of this from her. "Jesus, Haley. I'm so sorry I never told you about any of this. It was… it was so wrong of me." My eyes fall to the floor and I find it difficult to maintain eye contact with her.

"Stop it." She grabs my hands in hers. "Once this is settled and over with, you and I will sit down and discuss why you didn't tell me. But, for now, let's concentrate on helping Landon." She gives my hands a squeeze and lets out a deep breath as she scrutinizes me. "Now tell me everything you know." She's all business.

"All right." I glance at the two men on opposite sides of the living room. "But not here." I give Haley a look. "Let's go to my room."

"Fine." She stands, keeping a hold of one hand and tows me along with her.

We walk out of the living room, down the hallway to my bedroom.

I collapse on the bed as Haley lies down beside me. We both stare at the ceiling in silence for a moment. I sit up, cross my legs Indian style, and take a deep breath before I begin.

"After I returned home from Landon's," I briefly pause. "After… well, you know. Anyways, I came home and Agent Johnson showed up on my doorstep. He told me he was involved in an investigation concerning five men. He showed me pictures of the men. Haley…" I hold her gaze. "He had a picture of Landon, Alistair, and Jason. The other two men I've never seen before. I lied and told him I didn't know any of them, but when he left, Landon pulled into the driveway so he knew I was lying. I asked him why he was investigating them, but he wouldn't tell me anything. But…" I abruptly halt my story, wondering how to disclose the rest.

Haley sits up mirroring my position. "But?" she asks, impatiently.

"He told me Jason was dead." I grow quiet, expecting an explosive reaction from her, but when it doesn't happen, I continue. "Haley, at the time I thought… well, frankly, I thought Landon had something to do with it. I mean, Jesus Christ, Jason had just tried to rape me in Landon's club." I continue as tears sting my eyes. "What else was I supposed to think?"

"I get it." Haley grabs a hold of my hand. "It makes sense you would think that. Anyone would. But, Lexi… why didn't you come to me? That's what I don't understand. What did you think I would do?"

"I thought you would… that you would…" I take a deep breath. "I thought you would go nuts, make a scene. I don't know, but I knew you wouldn't let it go." My gaze falls to my lap knowing my actions are un-defendable.

"You would've been right because that's exactly what I would've done," she says, as she puts a finger under my chin and pulls my face up so we are eye to eye. "After I chopped his balls off and fed them to him." She winks.

I laugh.

Loudly.

Just the image of her with whips and chains.

Haley joins me in laughter as we fall back on the mattress. A silence settles around us as I stare at the ceiling, exhaustion over-powering me. It's been a long night. Turning my head, I glance at the clock on my nightstand. Five am. Shaking my head, I peek over at Haley.

"Let's get a little sleep," I suggest.

"I think that's a good idea." She moves to the top of the bed, crawling under the covers.

I follow her lead and inch up the bed. Laying my head on my pillow, I turn on my side to face Haley.

"Do you think this is going to work out?" I ask, a little more emotional than intended.

"Lexi, I hope so, for your sake." She runs her fingertips down my cheek. "I just want you to be happy."

"Me too," I whisper.

"Get some rest. We'll have clearer heads in the morning." She gives me a sad smile.

"Yeah. You're right." My eyelids close.

Bright morning sun shines through the window pulling me out of the darkness of sleep. I'm in shock I've managed any sleep at all, as I glance over at the alarm clock on the nightstand to see 8:00 illuminated in red. I got a solid three hours of sleep.

Stretching, I turn onto my side to see Haley sleeping peacefully. I don't want to wake her, so I roll back over, throw my legs over the side of the bed, my feet hitting the floor as I sit up.

Coffee.

I definitely need a strong cup of coffee today.

Because I'm dressed in the same outfit I had on last night, there's no need to change, so I leave the bedroom on my way to the kitchen.

Memories of last night bombard my mind. I briefly wonder if there will be men occupying my home as I continue down the hall and peer into the living room. Sure enough, there is one man standing in the hallway to the front door, and the other standing in the hallway which leads to the back door.

Groaning, I quickly duck back into the kitchen and begin my morning ritual of making coffee. Normally, I would make enough for two cups, but with the amount of people here, I decide to make a whole pot. After setting up the coffee maker, I lean back against the counter wondering what else I can do to pass time while I wait.

Going to one of the cupboards I pull out several mugs, putting them on the counter top. I move on to the fridge, pull out the cream, and then grab the sugar from its position next to the coffee maker. I place everything together on the counter. Shifting to a lower cupboard, I dig around for the serving tray I know is here, at last pulling it out too. I put everything onto the tray and place it on the island counter which separates the living room from the kitchen.

In this moment, I'm glad the partition is closed, allowing me some privacy from the men who are currently invading my living room.

The pot of coffee is half finished, so I think about what else I can do to keep busy. Food. That thought immediately comes to mind as I think of the men who are presently standing guard. *Surely, they must be hungry.*

I pull some bread out of the cupboard and toss four slices into the toaster. I know it won't be much, but I suppose something is better than nothing.

As the coffee finishes, I retrieve the pot and fill all the mugs. Just then, the toast pops up, so I remove those slices, setting them on a plate and put four more in.

I don't know how much these agents can eat, but they are pretty big guys, so I assume they eat a lot.

As I'm buttering the toast, Haley appears by my side.

"Do you need any help?" she offers as she yawns.

"No, I'm good. Would you like some coffee?" I point to a mug. "Toast will be ready in a second." I return to the task of buttering the toast.

Haley picks up a mug, adds some sugar, cream, and walks out of the kitchen.

I pull the partition open, revealing the living room just as Haley sits down on a stool on the other side.

I place the plate of toast on the serving tray just as the next batch pops up.

"Gentlemen, please help yourself to some coffee and toast." I offer the two men who haven't moved a muscle the entire time I've been here.

The agents, with stone-cold faces, glance at each other.

All is silent for several minutes before the agent standing by the front door shrugs his shoulders and mumbles, "Why not," before he walks over and grabs a mug of coffee.

My attention returns to the four pieces of toast still in the toaster and I begin the task of buttering them.

The silence in the room is eerie leaving me uncomfortable in my own home, the likes of which has never happened to me before. There are so many questions I want to ask, but recognize these men will never give me answers. It's apparent extracting any information from these two would be like pulling teeth.

Haley, on the other hand, has different plans.

"So." She clears her throat. "Why are you here?" she hisses at them. Or at least, I assume she is speaking to them, but with my back to her, I can't be certain.

I spin around to see her head swinging between the two agents waiting for an answer.

They stand on either side of her, as one is taking a bite of his toast, the other stirs his coffee. Both stop abruptly and peer down, inspecting Haley.

If we were in any other situation, this scene would be comical and I'm certain I'd be laughing my ass off at the sight of these enormous men with shocked expressions on their faces, peering down at little Haley. But, there is no humor in this situation and neither Haley nor the agents are budging.

"Are you going to tell me what is going on? Or, do I have to go to your superior?" she barks.

Both men examine her as if she has two heads.

Unexpectedly, the front door opens and all heads snap in that direction.

Agent Johnson waltzes in and instantly glances around

the room. Once he spots everyone at the counter he stalks toward us with a murderous look on his face.

Both agents drop their toast on the plate, and place their coffee mugs back on the counter top before turning to square off with Agent Johnson.

"Is this what I pay you for?" he growls at the two.

"Sorry, Sir. We were just..." Agent One's statement is left hanging as Agent Johnson cuts him off.

"This isn't a slumber party, Agent Simpson," Agent Johnson states through clenched teeth.

"Hey." My voice calls out against my wishes.

Everyone turns to stare at me, causing my face to heat up from embarrassment.

Silence surrounds us once more as the minutes tick by.

"Would you like a cup of coffee, Agent Johnson?" I offer casually hoping to break the tension. "Or perhaps some toast?" I wave my hand over the serving tray.

Instantly, all heads spin in the direction of Agent Johnson, waiting for his reaction. He's frozen with a grimace on his face as he assesses what I've said.

For an entire minute, which really feels more like an hour, he regards me before his face relaxes minutely. He steps forward, picks up a mug of coffee and proceeds to put sugar and cream in it.

Everyone watches as he picks up a slice of toast, bringing it to his lips, but before taking a bite he addresses the other agents.

"At ease gentlemen," he commands, then finally sinks his teeth into his toast.

The atmosphere in the room shifts bringing down everyone's anxiety level.

When the coffee is gone and the toast has disappeared, the two agents return to their posts.

Haley looks as if she's ready to pounce on Agent Johnson.

I decide to spare him her wrath.

"Agent Johnson, what is going on? Why are these men..." I point to his men. "...and you, in my house?" I attempt to keep my voice steady, although I'm anything but calm.

"Ms. Shaw, as I told you last night, *I* cannot discuss an ongoing investigation with *you*." His authoritative voice speaks volumes.

"Well, if that's all you have to say, then I see no reason for you to be here," I counter.

"Ms. Shaw, please. We're only trying to protect you," he reassures me.

"Protect her from what, exactly?" Haley interjects.

His head snaps in her direction and his eyebrows narrow as he scowls at her.

She glares right back, disgust taking over her features, but that can't be right, they don't even know each other.

"Ms. Rose, it will not do you good to take that tone with me. I am the law and will not tolerate your attitude," he warns, in a softer tone.

"My attitude." Haley jumps off the stool coming face to face with Agent Johnson. "You have some nerve waltzing in here, expecting us to jump at your command without telling us why."

"None of this is your concern or your business. You are free to leave anytime you wish," he seethes right back.

"Leave?" Haley laughs without humor. "I am not going anywhere and, Lexi... Is. My. Concern." She steps closer to Agent Johnson, pressing her forefinger into his chest. "If you think I'm leaving my best friend with the likes of you... think again. If you were any kind of a man, you would tell her *exactly* what is going on and *why* she is in danger. Until that's revealed..." She pushes her finger against his chest again for emphasis. "Until you tell her what the hell is going on...." She presses even harder, forcing Agent Johnson to stumble a little. "You're stuck with me." She steps back, resuming her seat on the stool.

Agent Johnson reins in his anger, appearing as though he may strike her otherwise. His face is red, hands balled into tight fists at his sides, eyes lingering on Haley who is calmly drinking her coffee as if nothing happened.

I freeze anticipating what the agent will do next. My eyes close as I think about what I'll do if he does strike her.

CHAPTER 3

*M*y eyes spring open as his voice breaks my reflection.

"I'm stopping for gas. We should get a few essentials before we get there?"

"Um..." I scan the area noticing a rundown old garage with a convenience store attached and I wonder if they'll have what we need. I'm also stunned we've driven this far already.

"Yeah, sure we'll need a few things." I undo my seatbelt.

He pulls beside a pump and pushes the car door open. Easing out of the vehicle he stands up and stretches.

This trip has been long. First, an eleven hour flight, then an hour and a half car ride. But, for me, time is frozen and it has no meaning anymore. Days—no weeks—have passed without notice. My only purpose is waiting for me at the end of this journey and nothing will stop me from solving the mystery that has become my life.

Finally, he pulls the vehicle down the long driveway of

the house we'll call home for however long we'll be here. My eyes sweep the grounds before he shifts the vehicle into park and my eyes meet his.

He pulls the door handle and hops out. I do the same, standing and stretching before glancing over at him. He gives me a pointed look before he strolls to the trunk and unloads our bags. Grabbing my suitcase and shoulder bag, I make my way to the front door.

He opens the door and steps over the threshold.

I pause, scanning the entire area before settling my sights on the castle across the way. There is the reason for my journey. That castle holds the secrets to unlocking the mystery that's been plaguing me since meeting Landon. I'm mesmerized by the beauty of it.

"Come inside," his voice pours out from somewhere in the house, shattering my daze.

I take a good look at the house, if you could call it that, it's more a cottage by American standards. We are in the middle of nowhere with no other houses for miles, the only thing in our vicinity is the castle—my main target.

Behind the walls of the castle that keep unwanted guests out, is my lifeline. I can feel it, almost taste it in the air that the bane of my existence is in there. At least that is my hope.

I have learned such a little amount about what is happening, or why on earth Landon is here in Italy, but there will be no rest until I bring him home.

As I position myself in front of the little window staring out at the walls that are keeping me from my life-line, I ponder how to get in and find what I'm looking for.

From the outside, the castle is magnificent with high stone walls, vast beautiful gardens, and what I believe is a vineyard. I wonder if they make their own wine. Lucky for me, our cottage is sitting on a hill giving me an unobstructed view the property. Although, there is little activity going on over there, I would assume wine making isn't on their list of priorities. It's also the wrong time of year for growing grapes.

I t's been a week since our arrival and there have been very few people coming and going from the place. They all resemble men you see in Mafia movies, wearing three-piece suits, covering their eyes with sunglasses and driving black SUV's. With little doubt, I know that whatever is happening on the other side of those walls is illegal.

The biggest red flag is the men who stroll the perimeter brandishing machine guns. The first day we arrived, it was a shock to see the first guard who was armed. I questioned whether Landon was even alive, but my counterpart reassured me. He reminded me that if Alistair's goal was to kill Landon he wouldn't have taken him in the first place. It sounded logical allowing hope to spring once again. But, my need to get him out of there has become urgent, and I will—one way or another.

There has been no visual of Landon—yet.

Still, I remain vigilant every day in front of this small window, hoping and praying for a glimpse. The need to see his face and know for certain he is here, alive and unharmed, is overwhelming. It would give me reassurance to know the weeks of preparation, the daily hounding and interrogations of anyone involved in Landon's situation, helped instead of hindering our progress.

I was ruthless in my pursuit of anything to do with Alistair, Jason or Landon's club. The worst it go was an FBI Agent call me callous and unforgiving because of my never-ending assault on their office. Needless to say, I was escorted from the building that day by Agent Johnson, who warned me that if I didn't change my behaviour he would throw me in a jail cell.

Like I cared.

I am ruthless and callous, but that's because people are treating me with kid gloves, trying to protect me when I'm not the one who needs protecting.

After that day, I was no longer allowed in the FBI offices. Not that I was disappointed much, because any information they had was not being offered to me. But none of it mattered. Regardless of how much they tried to keep me in the dark, the more passion I developed to gain information. What went beyond their comprehension, or they took for granted, was that I wasn't the naive, ignorant little woman they mistook me for. With my own connections, before long, I had launched my own investigation into Alistair.

"Any movement?" His voice wraps around me from behind.

I spin to see him smiling kindly at me.

"No. Nothing this morning." I turn back to the window.

"Don't worry Lexi." He wanders across the room to stand behind me. He places his hands on my shoulders giving them a gentle squeeze. "I'm sure it won't be long now."

"I'm not so sure about that." I'm completely unaware of my irregular breathing as a gust of air puffs out of my lungs. "What if we don't see him?" I whisper. "What if we never get confirmation that he's here? What do we do then?"

"Well, we'll move on to plan B."

After mentioning plan B, my attention returns to the morning following Landon's abduction because that's what it was—an abduction, and I refuse to think otherwise.

I close my eyes and think back to the big fight between Agent Johnson and Haley that morning.

CHAPTER 4

*A*fter opening my eyes, the standoff between Agent Johnson and Haley, ends peacefully, no blood shed, no more yelling.

Agent Johnson walks over to the agent by the front door and Haley remains at the counter sipping her coffee as if nothing at all happened.

I return to my bedroom while my thoughts run through my mind a mile a minute, making it hard to piece them all together.

Haley steps into the room and takes a seat beside me on the bed.

"Lexi, what can I do?"

"Bring him back," I stutter on the verge of tears.

She embraces me, squeezing tight. Finally, she holds me at arm's length, wipes her thumb under my eyes and gives me a small smile.

"That's what we'll do."

"What?"

"We'll get him back." She shrugs her shoulder.

"Just like that?"

"Yes," she sighs in exasperation. "Did you forget who I am?" She gives me a mischievous smirk.

"No." Although, I have my doubts there is anything she can do.

"Good. Remember, I know plenty of influential people in this town, who owe me favors. And, my parents have a huge rolodex that I'm not afraid to use. We'll find out what happened to him. I promise." Her sincerity is topped off by another hug.

"Now, what are we going to do about them?" She motions her hand toward the door.

"What about them?"

"Lexi, the FBI has taken up residency in your living room," she says with a 'duh' look on her face. When I don't answer immediately, she continues with a huff. "You can't just walk out of here." The aggravation is evident in her tone.

That's when it strikes me. I'm a prisoner in my own home. Haley's right. The agents in my living room aren't likely to let me waltz out of this house. They're here to protect me. From what? It's still unclear. The more I think about it, the angrier I become.

"What am I going to do, Haley? I'll never figure out where Landon is if I can't get out of here."

Haley gives my statement some consideration. "Why don't I head home and freshen up. I'll contact a few people while I'm there. See what I can find out. Then, when I

come back we'll figure out what to do about the Untouch-
ables in your living room."

I laugh. Out loud. It sounds weird to my own ears
causing me to stop as my eyes find Haley's.

"Okay."

With an expression of determination and a semi-quasi
plan in place, Haley springs from the bed and heads out of
the room. I follow her to the front hall.

Arriving at the door, she turns before opening it,
pulling me into another hug.

"I'll be back as soon as I can," she promises as she turns
the door handle, but before opening it she looks over her
shoulder. "We'll figure this out Lexi."

She pulls the door open, walks over the threshold and
closes it behind her.

I stare at the closed door, rationalizing what she's said
before spinning on my heels and heading back to my room.
There is no way I can deal with the uninvited captors in
my living room.

Collapsing onto the bed, my thoughts begin wandering
to how I ended up in this mess. Has it only been a couple
month since I ventured out to the club with Haley and
turned my life upside down? How could I get so wrapped
up in another man so soon after my divorce? Okay, it's
true, it wasn't quite after my divorce. What is wrong with
me turning to another man after being betrayed by my
husband? Why am I not more cautious, angrier by the
discovery of my husband's affair?

The sound of a car pulling into my driveway distracts
my thoughts.

I get up and walk over to my window to see who is arriving.

Agent Johnson steps out of his vehicle stretching to his full height.

The sun reflecting off the car blinds me, forcing my eyes to close.

CHAPTER 5

*O*pening my eyes, I stare out at the window to the driveway of the castle I've had my eyes glued to for the past week and a half. A car slowly proceeds up to the gate and comes to a halt. I watch as the gate opens and the car advances to the main doors. Two men dressed in black suits exit the vehicle and swiftly walk to the front door. Standing in the entryway is another man waiting to greet them before they all make their way inside.

I huff in aggravation wishing I knew who these men are, while facing the reality that I'll probably never find out.

"We'll make a visual," he says from his seat at the table where he is currently eating breakfast.

"How can you be so sure?" I spin around to glare at him. "What if he isn't here? What if we've been sitting here watching this place all this time and he isn't even here?" I complain for the thousandth time since arriving in Italy.

It's the same story with me, doubting everyone and

everything. I'm like a broken record. A week and a half of waiting patiently, well not exactly patiently, but waiting nonetheless, for some sign, a little reassurance, or any clue that Landon is behind the walls of that castle. And, for an entire week and a half nothing. Not one sign or indication that Landon is even here. I'm losing my patience. Hell, I'm going out of my mind! There's been no visual of Landon and none of Alistair either. The only people I've seen are the armed guards around the perimeter and a few others who look like errand boys that come and go from the place.

"Lexi, I've told you this many times." He gets up from the table and comes to stand behind me. My attention returns to the scene outside the window. "He's here, he has to be. Everything we know. Every piece of intelligence has led us here. They're here." He squeezes my shoulders in reassurance. "I can feel it." He squeezes one more time before letting go.

"I know, I can feel it too. I just wish we had more to go on. I just wish." I let out a breath of air. "I wish we'd see him." I turn around, offering him a look that lets him know he did his job once again.

Reassuring me is a daily event for him and he's extremely good at his job. Truthfully, it's surprising how understanding he is considering he never wanted me here in the first place.

Not everyone was on board with this trip, especially the man standing in front of me. He was adamant I remain in the States while he made the trip alone, but there was no way I would allow that. I worked too hard to find out everything I could about Alistair Marzano. I'm still full of questions and fearful of the answers, but that's what brought me here with a plan and a focus.

I return to my vigil of watching out the window paying special attention to the minions who come and go.

The sun reflects off the gate causes my eyes to close.

CHAPTER 6

*W*hen I open my eyes, I see Agent Johnson strolling toward my front door. I walk out of the bedroom heading into the living room as he saunters down the front hallway. When he steps into the living room he stops and glances at me. I'm praying he'll tell me something, anything, but his face is like a statue revealing nothing.

"What's happening? Did you find Landon?" I blurt out.

"Lexi?" Agent Johnson mutters.

"Tell me." I demand. "Tell me something. Please."

"There's nothing to tell," he says, in a firm voice.

I drop onto the couch trying to figure out what to do next.

Agent Johnson goes to each of his men and engages in whispered conversations. They aren't speaking loud enough for me to hear and it's annoying the hell out of me.

Determined, I get up, hurry to my desk in the corner of

the living room, and grab my laptop before walking in the direction of my bedroom.

Agent Johnson's loud voice calls out.

"Lexi."

I halt in my tracks and slowly turn to face him.

"What are you doing?" he growls.

His attitude is shocking at first, then appalling as I bark back my answer. "None of your business." I continue on to my bedroom.

I sense Agent Johnson rushing up behind me, but ignore his presence as I slip into my room. As I attempt to shut the door, he places his foot in the way, stopping me.

"What do you think you're doing?" I'm outraged by the audacity of this man.

"Stopping you from doing something stupid." He reaches forward and grabs a hold of my laptop.

I yank back and a game of Tug of War ensues.

We struggle for a few minutes before Agent One marches down the hall.

"What is going on here?" he asks.

We halt the struggle, but neither one of us lets go of the laptop.

"Agent Johnson, what are you doing?" Agent One inquires.

"Letting Lexi here know what the rules are," he replies, eyes boring into mine.

Rules!

Shock and disbelief course through me as I let go of the laptop, ready to give Agent Johnson a piece of my mind. Instantly, I realize my mistake as Agent Johnson quickly takes advantage by pulling the laptop away and handing it to Agent One, who withdraws quickly back down the hall with it.

Agent Johnson and I stand eye-to-eye waiting for each other to speak. There are so many things I want to say. Too many words running through my mind, none of which are rated PG, but he beats me to it.

"Lexi, please understand," his tone lightens drastically.

"Understand." I growl. "Understand, Agent Johnson."

I turn my back on him and head for my bed. Sitting down, I place my head in my hands, pulling my hair in frustration. This whole situation is utterly ridiculous. Is it really their intention to have me sit here doing nothing, going nowhere, and wait for them to say it's okay to resume my life? If that is Agent Johnson's intentions, he is sadly mistaken.

I hear a heavy sigh in the direction of the door. Tilting my head toward him, I see his shoulders slump, and a defeated look cross his features.

Am I winning?

Am I breaking him down?

"Tell me what is going on." I appeal to what I hope is a sign of weakness.

Agent Johnson looks ready to crumple as his face appears anguished. Then, just as quickly his mask slips back into place, letting me know the moment is lost.

"Lexi, you know I can't do that." He releases a breath of air. "If I could..." he pauses, drops his gaze to his feet before he squares his shoulders and meets my gaze. "I would tell you everything if I thought it would do any good. If I knew it wouldn't put you in danger." He crosses the room, taking the seat next to me on the bed. "But… I can't."

Even though I believe his words, I don't care. I'm angry… hurt… livid. It's hit the point of no return as I unleash everything on Agent Johnson.

"How dare you sit here and pretend that you're worried about my well-being." I say in an eerily calm demeanor. "You don't know me." I point to myself. "You don't know the first thing about me." I stand to face him, pointing my finger in his face.

"Don't tell me you're doing this for my own good. You're doing this so I won't screw up your investigation. You're doing this because you're wearing a badge and can get away with it. But let me tell you something, buddy. If you think I'm going to sit here like a good little girl and do everything you say," I lean in, coming face-to-face and eye-to-eye with him. "You've got another thing coming."

Agent Johnson doesn't move. I don't think he even blinks as he holds my glare. When he finally speaks, his tone is calm, gentle.

"Are you quite finished?" he asks softly.

"I haven't even started." I spit out with as much venom as possible.

"Look, I know you're upset. I know you're confused, but really Lexi, there's nothing I can tell you that will make you feel better. Can you at least try to be a little more understanding of my position here?" he pleads, which makes me want to rip his head off.

I want him to get angry, too. I want him to get mad,

yell, or scream. Instead, he sounds sorry, sincere even. I stand staring down at him for a minute before the second storm between the two of us brews stronger.

"Agent Johnson," I mutter. "I understand you have a job to do and I understand that your job may be keeping you from telling me what is going on." I pause for a moment collecting my thoughts. "But, I'm not part of your investigation. And, I refuse to be held prisoner in my own home," I inform him. "So either fill me in on what you know, or I'll be leaving now." I cross my arms over my chest in challenge.

He remains seated on my bed, holding my gaze.

"First of all, I am an agent for the Federal Bureau of Investigation." He stands to his full height leaning over me with anger swimming in his eyes. "I don't owe you any explanation. You will do as I say, or I will drag you from this house and place you under arrest. Do. I. Make. Myself. Clear?"

His eyes are bulging and I swear his eye color has gone from a soft sky blue to deep dark red.

I shrink away from his angry voice. I think I've finally pushed him too far. But, apparently my mouth and brain are not on the same page as the words fly out in a voice even I don't recognize.

"Arrest me. Arrest me. You've got to be kidding?" I chuckle without humor.

"Oh, I'm so not kidding. If you cause any more trouble for me or my officers, I will haul you in and keep you there indefinitely," he vows.

"You can't do that. I've done nothing wrong." I declare. "I know my rights." I add for good measure.

"Lady, your rights went out the front door the minute you called me," he hollers before taking a step back and a deep breath. "Look, Lexi, I'm sorry. I don't want to fight with you, but I'm telling you now that you are a part of this investigation. You're going to do as I ask, and believe me when I tell you, that it's for your own safety. I don't want to be in this position, but I am. So please, help me here."

I can only muster up one word to say to him. "Fine." I spit out, not liking the way the word sounds rolling off my tongue.

"What is going on in here?" Haley asks from outside my bedroom door, making both Agent Johnson and I snap our heads in her direction. "I could hear you two from the driveway," she adds.

"I was just leaving," Agent Johnson marches to the bedroom door as Haley strolls across the room to stand by my side. "Remember what I've said, Lexi."

"I said fine."

He nods his head then disappears out the bedroom door.

"What the hell was that all about?" Haley asks, frowning at the empty doorway.

"It would seem Agent Johnson and I don't see eye-to-eye on a few issues." I collapse onto the bed.

Haley sits down beside me, studying me for a moment.

I stare up at the ceiling, going over my conversation with Agent Johnson, trying to make sense of it all, but can't. Instead, my attention shifts to Haley who is staring at me with concern in her eyes.

"He won't let me leave," I announce, letting out a gust of air.

"What?" she asks, confusion written all over her face.

I sit up locking gazes with her. "He won't let me leave, use my computer..." I pause as I think about everything he said. "I'm not even sure if I can use my phone," I utter, mostly to myself before I reach over to the nightstand and grab the phone from its cradle. Clicking the talk button I get my answer. I let out another puff of air, defeated. "It's dead," I whisper.

"Yeah, I figured as much," Haley says nonchalantly by my side.

"What?"

"I tried to call you earlier." She shrugs. "I figured they cut the phone lines when the recording said your line was out of service. Then I tried your cell phone half a dozen times, but it kept going to voice mail. That's why I came back so quickly. I wanted to make certain you were okay."

She pulls me into her, squeezing me tight.

Except, I'm not all right. I'm far from it, but have no idea what to do next.

I hug her back, trying to absorb some of her strength. She was always the stronger one of our duo, and right now I want her strength more than I ever have before. The truth is, if I had to do this on my own, I would lay down in this bed, and pull the covers over my head until this whole nightmare is over. Forgetting everything would be bliss right now. Unfortunately, that's not in the cards for me.

Landon is out there... somewhere, mixed up with a lunatic, and whether or not I develop a future with this man, I feel compelled to help him. There's a twisting in my stomach and a tug in my chest warning me that something is very wrong. I know I need to help him. How I do that, I have no idea, but I have to find a way.

I pull back from the hug as curiosity engulfs me.

"Did you find out anything?" I'm almost fearful of her answer.

"Well, two things are certain. One, Alistair Marzano is one very corrupt man. Two, whatever you stumbled into here is bigger than either of us realize," she reveals quietly so the other Agents don't hear.

I fix my gaze on her, waiting for an explanation.

"Look Lexi, I'm not going to lie to you. This is some heavy duty shit were talking about. From what I've been able to learn this morning, this Alistair Marzano is like the king of crime around these parts. He's associated with everything from drugs, to girls, to God knows what else. He owns whorehouses all over town and there are plenty of people who work for him. As for the connection between Landon and him..." She pauses as she stares straight into my eyes, letting me see her fear. "I have no idea," she admits in defeat. "There's nothing."

It's difficult to see Haley in this state. Fear is not something I've witnessed from her often, but it's clear as day on her right now. This should give me pause. It should make me reconsider what we're doing here, but it doesn't, so I push forward.

She has to be wrong... There has to be something.

Somebody knows something. Why else would Landon just walk away with him like that?

As realization strikes, me I gasp.

Haley glances at me, confused. "What is it?"

"You don't think," I pause.

"What? Lexi, I don't think what?" she asks anxiously.

"You don't think Landon is involved in Alistair's business?" I ask in a low voice, remembering the ears that are lingering in my house.

Haley appears deep in thought as my mind wanders too. My thoughts take on a different twist as I begin planning my escape. I close my eyes trying to figure out the best way out of here.

CHAPTER 7

s I open my eyes and gaze out at the view I have memorized for the past week, I know this has brought me one step closer to solving this mystery.

After all my investigating, I came away with a bunch of useless information. Sure, I know who I am dealing with and some of the crimes Alistair has been accused of. I know he's a murderer, he admitted as much that night in my living room. However, I'm no closer to figuring out why Landon agreed to go with him. Why he walked out my front door, on a leash no less, is still a mystery.

Looking out at the vast lands that surround the castle, I'm still in the dark about who those people are and what they are doing with Landon. I'm not even convinced that he is somewhere within the walls of that compound.

As I survey the grounds for what feels like the millionth time since arriving here, one of the doors at the side of the castle swings open. It's the first time I've seen that door in use and it holds my attention captive.

A huge man, wearing combat gear and holding a machine gun, steps over the threshold, swinging his head left and right as he glances all around as if he's looking for something... or someone.

My heart slams into my chest as the man stares straight at the window I'm standing in front of. Instinctively, I duck to the side out of view of the window, back pressed against the wall. It's absurd to think he can tell who I am from that distance, but since arriving here, I'm constantly being badgered about exposing myself. My comrade continually reminds me to stay hidden, never revealing who we are or what we look like. It's unclear if I'm recognizable, and he's not about to take any chances. His words not mine.

If things were my way, we would have walked right up to that castle and demanded entry the day we arrived. I suppose that's why he's the professional, and up until now, I've listened and went along with his requests.

Sneaking a peek out the window, I see the man has come further out into the open.

Another man, also large in stature and wearing combat attire, but sans a gun, has joined him. They glance all around the surrounding area then converse with one another. These men appear casual, as one man laughs wholeheartedly, and the other man slaps him on the shoulder. A second later, the first man waves his hand at the door, motioning for whoever is on the inside to come out.

My breath stops. My chest clenches. And, my world starts spinning. My brain no longer functions when I catch sight of a man who stumbles out the door. He covers his eyes with his hands as if the sun is burning them. I know immediately who it is even though the changes in him are immense. There's not a shadow of a doubt that this is my reason for being here. This is the reason I have flown half way around the world. Only one word escapes my lips.

"Landon." His name comes out as a breathless whisper as I press my hands against the window.

A strong tug around my torso is pulling me away from the vision in front of me. I struggle against his hold, as one hand covers my mouth and the other pulls me to his chest from behind.

Shocked and stunned, I give up the fight and listen to his rambling.

"Lexi, stop. They'll hear you," he exclaims anxiously, while restraining me.

It's not until then I realize I'm sobbing uncontrollably, making noises I've never made before. The sound is an awful wailing, shocking me to my core and silencing me abruptly. Taking a deep cleansing breath, I brush away the wetness from under my eyes. I plant my feet firmly on the ground and grab his hands, freeing myself.

"I'm okay," I murmur softly. "I'm fine. I'm sorry." He lets me go and I turn to face him. "I'm sorry, it won't happen again." I wipe away more of the offending tears.

He gives me a nod before stepping around me to glance out the window. He stands to the left as I shift to the right. We peek out together to get a glimpse of what is happening.

Landon stands between the two giant men, his head tilted back as he gazes up to the sky. He is basking in the warmth of the sun.

I snatch up the binoculars for a better view. Landon is wearing pajama bottoms and nothing else. He is barefoot and bare-chested. As my eyes travel up his body I notice his weight loss, or I believe he has lost weight because his muscles don't appear as big as they were. But, my view point may be skewed by the two men standing next to him. They really are enormous.

His hair is a mess, even messier than normal, and he has the makings of a full-grown beard. He looks so different from the strong, confident man I know from his club. He looks... Well, he looks broken.

My heart aches as the urge to grab him and run away overwhelms me. Standing here and peering out the window at him is the most difficult thing I've ever done in my life. I'm not supposed to draw any attention to us and that is proving to be harder than I ever imagined.

We watch in silence as the three men stand in the sun for half an hour before they head back inside.

I take a deep breath and I move away from the window.

"He's here." I exclaim at last.

"Yes, he's here," he repeats with a broad smile on his face and a little bit of vindication showing.

I smile back, but it feels wrong. Smiling, while I know Landon is in pain is just plain wrong.

"Hey, don't do that," he whispers. "We found him, be proud. It's okay to feel good about that," he reassures me before squeezing my shoulder and stepping away. "Now, the real work begins." His smile widens.

"Yes, it does," I agree wholeheartedly.

The next three days are spent watching Landon spend

time outside at exactly the same time and for precisely half an hour. He strolls out the door guarded by the same two goons. He saunters over to a tree where he sits down, his back leaning against the trunk. He looks better than the first day we saw him. Every day spent outside appears to do wonders for him. By the third day, he has shaved, giving an unobstructed view of his beautiful face. He tilts his head toward the sky for about fifteen minutes of his time. After, he walks around in small circles, kind of strolling.

A week after the first sighting, his two goons have been reduced to one. The guard stands leaning against the wall fiddling with his phone. He pays no attention to Landon until it's time to head back inside.

Landon continues his daily strolls and his circle expands in size everyday as he enjoys the sun.

While I've been watching him intently for days, my partner spends a lot of time on his computer and phone, but I never pay attention. I'm too busy planning Landon's escape. Every day I watch him come out and every day my heart breaks watching him disappear back through the door.

We are wasting time sitting around waiting.

"When are we going to make our move?" I stomp my foot as I glare over at my comrade.

"You already know the answer to that, so stop asking me." He doesn't even glance at me, instead keeping his attention focused on his computer.

Damn it. The wait is killing me.

I return to the view out the window.

Landon seems agitated. His head is bobbing up and

down and his lips are moving very fast. I glance over at his bodyguard to see he's still against the wall, not paying one ounce of attention to Landon.

I grab the binoculars off the table next to me and hold them in front of my eyes to secure a better view. Landon's lips are moving fast and now he is running both hands through his hair, a gesture I know well. There is definitely something wrong with him.

"Come here and take a look at this," I call over my shoulder.

I hear shuffling behind me before he is standing next to me with his own pair of binoculars.

We watch in silence for a moment or two.

"What do you think he's doing?" I ask, dying of curiosity.

"I'm not sure..." he says quietly, then pauses for a moment. "If I had to guess..." He stops again, pausing before replying. "I would think he is talking to someone?" It's more of a question than an observation.

"That's exactly what I thought, but who could he be taking to? That guy over there isn't even looking at him. And Landon's got his back to him." I watch Landon's hand run through his hair again. "He's definitely agitated. Something's wrong with him." I lower my binoculars and glance at my comrade.

"I know," he mutters keeping his binoculars level with his eyes.

Quickly, he places them on the table as he rushes out of the room.

I watch his retreating form.

"Where are you going?" I'm met with silence. "What are you doing?" I glare at the door he exited through.

He struts back in setting a black box on the table, pulling out a cord from the back of it and plugs it into the wall. It looks like an old scanner my father used to listen to on his days off. He would listen to what was happening with his police officers from our living room.

I glance at the box on the table, then at the man fiddling with it. He is concentrating on the scanner.

"Is he still talking?" he asks, as he glances at me.

I spin back to the window raising the binoculars to my eyes.

"Yeah, but he doesn't look agitated anymore." I watch Landon's lips move.

I hear a crackling sound and what I would refer to as white noise fills the room as he flips through channels on the scanner.

And then I hear it. The voice I've been dying to hear for weeks.

Landon's voice fills the silent space and I turn quickly to glare at the scanner.

"...it has to be done," Landon pauses for a moment before continuing. "There's nothing I can do about it. You're just going to have to trust me."

Another voice fills the air, this one I know too.

"I don't like it. It's too dangerous. What if?" Landon's driver is cut off.

"I know, but it's the only way. I need radio silence tonight. I'll power off at six this evening and be back on at seven in the morning, understood?"

"Yes, Sir, but…" Lawrence replies before being cut off again.

"Look, I know you don't like radio silence, but it's necessary. We'll talk more tomorrow. Got to go," Landon ends the conversation.

"Take care, Mr. Miller."

I glance out the window once again watching as Landon tilts his face at the sun and takes a few deep breaths.

The guard standing against the wall straightens to his full height. His voice comes through the scanner.

"Times up."

Landon strolls over to the guard and through the open door, the guard follows him. The door slams shut and the sound of footsteps fills the room, boots on tiled floor it sounds like. Another door opens.

"He wants you ready at seven sharp," the guard growls at whom I assume is Landon.

The door slams shut.

Silence fills the room and I peek at my comrade.

"What do you think that's all about?" I ask.

"I'm not sure, but one thing is for certain—that other guy doesn't like what's about to happen." He looks puzzled, concerned.

"What time is it?" I wonder how long until radio silence.

"Going on four. We have two hours."

We listen for a few minutes to dead air.

"I guess he's alone." I move to take a seat at the table.

"Sounds like it," he whispers back. "But this is good.

Now we can hear what is going on in there." He glances at me seeing the uncertainty that I'm sure is well displayed. "It will be easier to rescue him if we know what we're dealing with," he explains.

"I know." My focus returns to the scanner. "That was his driver, Lawrence, by the way," I offer.

"What?"

"Landon's driver. That's who the other voice is." I glance at him. "He drove me home from the club a couple of times. I would know his voice anywhere," I explain remembering all the times I was at the club and realizing how stupid and naive I truly am.

I've had my suspicions about Landon's employees. As far as knowing who they truly are and what they do, there was no way I could tell from the few encounters I've had with them.

That's another habit I've formed in the past few weeks —*blaming* myself for being naive. If I hadn't gone with Jason in the first place, none of this would be happening. Blaming myself for Landon's situation has become a daily occurrence since this whole nightmare began.

"Hey, don't do this again." His voice jars me from my self-loathing thoughts.

"I'm not."

He glares back at me, raising an eyebrow.

"Fine, I'm stopping."

I focus back on the scanner, listening and praying to hear Landon's voice again.

For the next two hours, I remain glued to my chair with

all of my concentration aimed at the little black box sitting on the table in front of me. There are very few sounds and absolutely no talking. I had hoped to hear his voice, but he never speaks.

At first, I think he's sleeping or perhaps reading, but at five o'clock I hear movement in the room. I struggle to figure out what he is doing, but with no visuals, it's pointless, so I keep listening to the small noises he's making.

At five thirty, I hear water running, most likely the shower, so I assume he is getting ready, for what I have no idea. But, I do know that my time listening is almost up. Landon mentioned radio silence would begin at six o'clock sharp and he is definitely a man of his word.

An ache in my chest forms.

We finally have confirmation that he's here. This also gives us the opportunity to figure out why he's here, which can only help to get him out. However, as quickly as that breakthrough comes, it seems to be slipping away just as fast.

"It's going to be okay," he says from his position across the room.

He's typing furiously on his laptop and has been since we found the channel Landon's been using. I have no clue what he is doing because I've been unable to take my eyes off the scanner.

A click sounds from the black box, then absolute silence.

"What time is it?" I shriek rattling him.

"Six," he informs me before removing his fingers from

the keyboard, rising from his chair and making his way across the room to sit next to me.

"It's going to be all right."

I close my eyes trying to disappear for a few minutes.

CHAPTER 8

I open my eyes and break away from Haley's embrace. Standing up from the bed, I wander over to the window to peek out. It's a beautiful day, the sun is shining giving off a warm glow. The kind of day you want to spend entirely outside. The street it's quiet, peaceful and I'm certain my house looks the same. Appearances sure are deceiving. That's the true mystery of life. How can everything appear one way, but actually be the complete opposite? I'm certain anyone walking by this house would view it as a picture perfect. Little would they know my entire world is falling apart, or that I am being held hostage.

"I have to get out of here." I eye Haley over my shoulder.

"How?" She studies me with one eyebrow arched.

"I don't know yet, but I'm not going to sit around here and wait for... whatever they're going to do." I jab my thumb in the direction of the living room. "Haley?" I march over to her and resume my seat beside her on the bed. "They think Landon is some sort of criminal. They think he's associated with Alistair, but you and I were there. We know that's not true, right?" I hold my breath waiting for her answer, praying she's on my side.

"You're right, Lexi. Landon's not involved in any of this. I'm not sure why he went with Alistair, but I know he's not a criminal. From the bit of information I've been able to gather this morning, he's an upstanding businessman in this community. Everyone praises the man. So, none of this makes sense. Rest assured, I'll help you in any way I can. We'll get to the bottom of this." She pulls me into an embrace. "Okay?"

"Thank you. And, Haley?" I squeeze her tightly before letting go. "I'm sorry I dragged you into this mess."

"Lexi, you didn't drag me into this. In fact, as I recall, *I* dragged you into this mess."

"You know what?" I stand up turning to face her head on. "You're right, you did drag me into this. This…" I wave my hand at the door to my bedroom dramatically, "…is all your fault," I finish keeping my face straight.

Haley peeks up at me, eyes wide, concern splashed across her features, and because I can no longer hold back, I burst out laughing.

Haley joins in and we collapse on the bed, our backs hitting the mattress with a thud. We lay, giggling to each other as I regain a little hope that this situation will come out in my favor. It may be false hope, but at this point, I'll take it. Our laughter dies down.

"How the hell am I going to get around the agents in my

living room?" I stare at the ceiling trying to formulate a plan of escape.

"You know, you've done nothing wrong. They're not charging you with anything. Therefore, they really have no reason to hold you here."

I let my head fall to the side and gaze at her. She's right. They have no right to hold me here against my will.

With a renewed burst of energy, I jump off the bed and head to my closet to dress for the day.

"Where are you going?"

"I'm getting ready to get out of here." I enter my closet to pick out an outfit. "Are you coming with me?" I peek out the closet door to look at her.

"And miss the confrontation about to happen in the living room? Of course. This, I've got to see." A wicked smile spreads across her face.

I can almost feel what it must be like to be Superman when he steps into the phone booth to put on his world-saving suit. Unfortunately, for me, it's not as easy to pick out a life-saving outfit. Honestly, my wardrobe doesn't measure up, or even come close, if there's such a thing as a world saving suit. Instead, I settle on a pair of cream-color khakis, a white button-down shirt with a pair of flats. Then, it's off to the bathroom to brush my hair and teeth.

The entire time I'm getting ready I think about where to start investigating. If my goal is to find out more about Alistair, the smart move would be to start where we first made contact. That means heading back to Landon's club. I assume Leroy won't let us in. I'm hoping he won't be there, or at the very least, he'll be too busy trying to help Landon to notice us.

Most of this will be a moot point if I can't get out of this house. My thoughts turn to the men occupying my living room as the time to see where my fate stands arrives. I wander out of the bathroom, presenting a stronger front than I'm actually feeling.

Haley rises from her seat on my bed, strong and confident as usual. I don't know how she does it, but she's always been sure of herself. I envy her self-assurance.

She flashes a smile knowing it's exactly what I need for the task ahead.

Presenting a united front, we walk out of my room, down the hall, and into my living room.

I'm surprised to see Agent Johnson lingering at the breakfast bar, phone to his ear, engrossed in conversation. Truthfully, I thought he had left after our earlier encounter.

I almost spin around and walk back to my room, but Haley places her hand on my shoulder urging me forward. I walk over and stand next to the agent, waiting patiently for him to finish his call. Once he presses the end button I seize my opportunity.

"I am going out for a while with Haley." I confront him in a tone I don't recognize.

"Lexi?" Agent Johnson expels a breath of air.

He stands to his full height, squaring his shoulders. "I'm afraid I can't let you do that."

"You can't or you won't?" I challenge him.

"I can't protect you if you're not here."

"Protect me from what?"

Agent Johnson gets off the stool and paces the floor in front of me.

I glance at Haley who shrugs her shoulders.

I return my attention back to Agent Johnson.

He's pacing back and forth mumbling to himself. Any attempt to hear what he is saying is useless. Finally, he spins to face me head on.

"Look. There's a lot of things happening right now and I can't, in good conscience, have you running around town unprotected. You need to stay here until we have things under control."

"Am I under arrest?" I ask, maintaining a strong voice.

"What? No. Don't be ridiculous." He dismisses my question with a wave of his hand.

"Am I under suspicion, you know, like don't leave town or anything like that?" I'm dead serious.

"Lexi?"

"So you have no right to hold me here. Right?"

"It's not about—"

"Right?"

"Yes. You're right. But, I'm begging you to reconsider. If you ask us to leave… If you walk out that door… we'll be gone and we're not coming back. Trust me when I tell you, you want our protection, you need our protection and we can't protect you if you won't let us," he cautions maintaining his authority.

I hesitate, giving thought to what he's saying. If I'm being completely honest, I'm afraid, more terrified than I've ever been in my entire life. However, I'm not about to let fear rule this situation. The only thing I know for certain is that someone I love is out there, on his own, and in trouble. I have to help him. I have to find him and bring him home.

I realize the FBI won't be including me in their investigation. It's also evident that Leroy and Landon's crew won't be sharing anything with me either. In order to figure out what is happening, and where Landon is, I'll be on my own. That much is evident.

I glance at Haley who shrugs her shoulders again, with an added eyebrow hike, offering me her approval to decide our position. Her expression reassures me that she will remain by my side regardless of my verdict. The outcome isn't surprising. In truth, there really is no choice.

Turning back to Agent Johnson, I can read the defeated demeanor in his body language before I reveal my decision.

"Thank you for trying to protect me, but your services are no longer needed."

I spin on my heels, stroll over to the end table next to the couch, grab my purse and head for the front door. In the foyer, I grab my car keys from the bowl perched on top of the side table before stepping through the door, pausing long enough to shout to Haley.

"You coming?" I don't wait for her response as I stroll down the stairs toward my vehicle.

The sound of Hailey's footsteps rushing up behind me has me smiling before she falls into step at my side.

"Lexi?" She grabs my arm, halting my steps forward.

As I turn to glance at her, I doubt my decision for a split

second. Her face lights up in a bright smile, aiming pride at me before her smile changes to a smirk.

"Let's take my car," she says already heading in that direction.

I'm just as proud of myself for displaying the courage to stand up to Agent Johnson.

My pride lasts a short stint as dread washes over me and panic sets in when I realize what I've just done. I quickly recognize the impact of not having the agents around to protect me. *What if Agent Johnson is right? What if I just put me and everyone I know in danger?* It's clear that Alistair is a murderer. I don't know all the details, but he did confess to murdering Jason.

I open the passenger door to Haley's car and plop down into the seat as all of the confidence I exhibited only moments ago rushes out of me. I question every decision made in the last twenty four hours.

"You did the right thing." Haley squeezes my hand no doubt grasping the uncertainty plaguing my mind.

She turns the key in the ignition, puts the car into gear pulling away from my house. I peek back and notice how peaceful and quiet it looks from the street. None of my neighbors will ever know what is really happening under that roof.

I close my eyes in an attempt to gain some perspective on the situation.

CHAPTER 9

*O*pening my eyes, the only thing I can see is the little black box, which has become an essential part of my daily routine.

Thirteen hours of radio silence is as dreadful as death. It's identical to losing him all over again, with the exception of knowing he is within my grasp. There's nothing I can do but sit and wait. Last night was spent in agony fighting the urge to march over there and bust the door down. That is the exact reason my comrade never intended to bring me on this trip. He told me in the beginning that my emotional attachment to the situation could have catastrophic consequences. I told him to drop dead.

My evening was devoted to travelling between the window and the scanner.

My comrade spent the evening at his desk doing God knows what. The less he appeared to do the more enraged I grew. It wasn't my plan to come all this way to sit here and watch. We came here on a mission. Well, I'm here on a mission and that is to get Landon back. I still have no idea how my comrade ended up in all of this. He's still a mystery to me. He's never shared with me why he's here. Or, why he has such an invested interest in this particular situation.

Early on, none of that mattered to me. I needed help and he was the only one willing to help me. I needed him.

Scrutinizing him now, has me curious to know his story. *What brought him here? Why did he go out of his way to help me? Or, Landon for that matter?* I decide the only way to kill my curiosity is to find out why he agreed to come here.

"Agent Johnson?" I saunter over to his desk.

"Lexi, how many times do we have to have this conversation?" he interjects with a smile. "The name's, Dalton." He reminds me for the billionth time.

"Fine. Dalton. Why are you here?" I deadpan.

"You know why I'm here."

"No. What I mean is, you've never told me why you're so invested in this case. Why Landon?"

Dalton rubs his forefinger along his temple as he lets out an exaggerated sigh. He stands up from his chair, completely ignoring me, as he walks by on his way to the kitchen. He pulls open the fridge, grabs out two beers, than walks back over, holding one out to me.

I grab the bottle and watch as he wanders over to the couch and plops down. I follow his actions, taking the seat next to him. We open our beers, both taking a long pull. He doesn't drink often, stating he is here for a reason. And being alert, ready to handle any situation, comes with the territory.

As I watch him take another swallow, I begin to doubt whether knowing his story is worth the stress it appears to cause him.

"When I was new to the bureau I was sent on assignment here in Italy. I worked at the American Consulate for a period. It was mostly surveillance and boring. One night, while working the night shift in my office, I had cameras in there and could see the entire building.

"Anyways, this young man walks in and heads straight to the front desk. He immediately caught my attention. His body language told me he was scared to death, but he didn't seem to be portraying that while talking to the guard. My curiosity got the better of me and I went out to the hall to hear what was going on. The young man kept looking behind him, out the door as if he were looking for someone. From the conversation he was having with the guard, it seemed as if he lost his passport and all his belongings. He had no way to get home." Dalton glances at me.

I nod my head encouraging him to continue.

"I knew immediately something was wrong with him so I approached them, cautiously. The guard glanced at me, indicating he knew there was something wrong too, so I stepped in to offer my assistance. I introduced myself and offered my hand to the young man. He hesitated at first, but grasped my hand with a timid shake. I told him to come to my office so we could resolve his issues.

"He looked out the front door, and again, I wondered who he was looking for, then he began walking. Together we went down the hall to my office. I told the guard on duty to stand by and wait for further instructions. Although, I knew this boy was in trouble something told me that he wasn't about to attack the place. I opened the door to my office and ushered him in, closing my eyes and taking a deep breath." Dalton takes another pull from his beer before continuing.

He shuts his eyes and begins telling the story as if he's reliving the memory in his mind.

CHAPTER 10

*A*s I open my eyes I watch the young man standing in my office practically shaking in his shoes and my heart clenches.

What is wrong with this kid?

"Please, have a seat." I close my office door and walk to the other side of my desk taking my own seat.

The boy is extremely timid and awfully nervous. My gut advises me to get to the bottom of this quickly.

"So." I decide a friendly atmosphere is probably the best approach. "Were you robbed?"

"You could say that." His voice is so soft it's almost a whisper.

I stare at him, trying to assess him and the situation. His head is tilted downward, hands folded together resting on his lap, and he hasn't moved a muscle since taking the seat. But, the most disturbing behavior is his refusal to make eye contact.

"You want to tell me want happened?" I invite in a soft voice, afraid to rattle him more than he already is.

"Not really," he answers in a whisper, making me strain harder.

It's quite apparent something terrible has happened to him, igniting my need to find out more about his situation. But, before I have a chance to ask, he steels himself, sits up straight in the chair. He glances up at me making eye contact for the first time and speaks in the strongest voice I've heard from him yet.

"Look, I just want to go home." He looks me straight in the eye.

A thousand emotions cross his face before he settles on determination. He holds my gaze for as long as he can before it's too much for him and he lowers his head once more.

My chest aches as I witness his facial expressions go from determination to horror in a matter of a couple of seconds. It's highly evident that I need to gain control of the situation as fast as I can before he shuts down completely.

"Okay, let's start with where is home?"

"The United States," he says quickly.

I smirk at the obviousness of his answer—his accent giving him away—even though he is terrified he still has some defiance in him. There is something about his smart remark that makes me smile.

"Where in the United States?"

"Seattle," he proclaims.

Seattle strikes a chord with me. There's something about Seattle that settles in my mind, something I should know but can't quite remember. I think for a second to see if it'll come to me, but for the life of me I can't remember. Giving up, I continue my attempt to solve the mystery of the boy in front of me.

"Can you tell me your name?" I pull out a pad and pen from my drawer and begin writing the information down.

"Landon." He purposely omits his last name.

This is definitely going to be a long night.

"Landon. Okay." I take a deep calming breath before continuing. "Here's the thing Landon, I can't help you if you won't talk to me."

Landon doesn't budge. He's as still as a statue.

I'm getting irritated and wondering how to help someone who doesn't want help. I believe our normal tactics in the FBI of dealing with unaccommodating people, extracting the truth by any means necessary, won't work with this young man. He's different. I know that interrogating him, or hassling him will only serve to shut him down more than he already is. I have to handle him carefully, so I change my approach.

As I write his first name on the pad of paper in front of me, I blurt out my next question. "Last name?" I pray he'll just let it slip out.

He moves slowly raising his head to glare at me.

"Miller." He holds my gaze for a second before lowering his head once again.

His name sounds so familiar it startles me. I wonder

why his name together with Seattle, makes me think I'm missing something here. His actions while stating his last name are not normal. He looked me square in the eye as if he were looking for something—recognition maybe.

Unfortunately, nothing comes to mind as I stall while running it around my mind for a second. His name, combined with the city, leaves me with a troubled feeling about the whole situation.

With a name and a city, I have enough information to run a search. Since talking to him isn't accomplishing anything, I drum up an excuse to leave the room.

"Landon?" I'm hoping he'll look at me. Sadly he doesn't. "I'm going to start the process of getting you a new passport."

I get up from my chair, stroll over to the door, reach out to grab the handle and give it a turn before looking back at the young man. "I'll be right back," I promise. Still, there's no reaction from him.

I walk out the door, closing it behind me and lean against it. Taking a deep breath, my shoulders relax and I'm just now realizing how tense it is in that room. After a couple more deep breaths, I push off from the door and head over to the front desk.

"Everything okay Boss," the night guard asks with an expression of concern on his face.

"I'm not sure, Jerry. Something's not right. What did he say when he came in?"

"Not much before you came out. He just asked how he could get a new passport. Said he lost his," he responds.

"Not that it was stolen or missing?" I question wondering which story is the truth.

"Nope, he definitely said he lost it. Then you walked out here," he replies. "What's his story?"

"I'm not sure. Do me a favor?" I slide the piece of paper I'm holding across the counter. "This is his name and the city he's from. Find out everything you can about him and bring it to me on the down low. Okay?" I turn to walk back to my office.

"Sure, boss," Jerry replies, as I slip back through my office door.

Landon hasn't moved a muscle since my departure. He sits perfectly still with his hands in his lap, head down. It's alarming to see him this way.

Most people I encounter in this office are hardcore, rough, and tough even. It's rare to see someone so docile in my line of work. His whole demeanor is throwing me off.

Calmly, I return to my desk, collapse in my chair and look at the young man in front of me. He can't be more than twenty. He appears scared and hesitant. I want to know his story. I need to know what brought him here. Erring on the side of caution, I decide to start with something simple.

"Are you here on vacation?"

"Not exactly."

"Visiting family?" I try again.

"No."

"Then can you tell me why you are in Italy?" Each piece of the puzzle will bring me closer to solving this mystery.

Silence. I'm met with nothing but silence causing me

some anxiety. I glare at him for a few minutes, giving him time to respond. He remains motionless with his head down and hands folded on his lap. *What the hell is wrong with this guy?*

Letting out a puff of air, I make another attempt. "Landon, I can't help you if you don't tell me what's wrong?"

There are a few more moments of silence.

"I told you already, I lost my passport and wallet." He talks so quietly I have to lean forward in my seat and strain to hear him. "I just want to go home."

A knock on my office door startles me.

"Come in." I yell out, thankful for the interruption.

Jerry opens the door, steps in and walks over to my desk, dropping a file down. He stands examining Landon for a moment, then turns back to me. He raises an eyebrow, but I shrug him off.

"Thanks, Jerry." I snap letting him know to vacate the room.

"No problem." He walks back to the door, opens it, but turns to glance at Landon studying him for a moment. He turns and leaves, closing the door behind him.

I open the file, glancing over the information. And, there it is, the reason Landon's name bothered me so much. The first paper is a report about a missing college student from Seattle, Landon Miller. Shock courses through me as I read on. He went missing a year ago. No clues were found, no ties to anything drug related and no crime scene found. Landon Miller just disappeared one night without a trace. Flipping through the papers quickly,

I realize he was never found... Yet, here he sits across from me begging to go home.

Where the hell has this kid been?

I close my eyes for a moment trying to think of what to do next.

CHAPTER 11

"*H*oly shit." I roll my head sideways on the couch to peer at Agent Johnson who has his eyes closed as he paints me a picture of how he met Landon at least fifteen years ago. "What happened to him? Where had he been all that time?" I ask, bewildered by this revelation.

Dalton slowly opens his eyes and rolls his head on the back of the couch to peer at me.

"Well, as for what happened to him," Dalton pauses. "That's not my story to tell. But, as for where he had been all that time…" He stands up, drifts over to the window and glances out at the castle we have been watching since our arrival.

"Oh my God. He was here. But, why?" I'm confused again.

"There's a lot you don't know and a lot I can't tell you," Dalton whispers while his attention remains out the window.

I wait, hoping he will elaborate further, but he stays silent as my thoughts race with this new information.

Landon was here when he was missing?

Why here?

Why now?

None of this makes sense. It's hard for me to imagine Landon involved with these criminals. He was only twenty-one at the time of his disappearance. Maybe, he got involved with the wrong people. Reckless kid stuff that never went away. These seem like the type of people that would be hard to shake. That has to be it. Landon must have some sort of obligation to them.

Does that mean Landon is one too?

Oh God, what if I'm here, risking everything to help a criminal?

"What exactly is Landon's involvement with these people?" I hesitate, afraid to hear the answer.

"Lexi, I've told you this a thousand times..." Dalton spins around to face me. "It's not my story to tell."

His position is complicated, but we are talking about some of the biggest gangsters on the planet. I have every right to demand full disclosure. I've put my entire life on hold, and evidently on the line, to pursue this.

Am I not entitled to truth?

Am I not entitled to know whether or not I'm helping someone on the wrong side of the law?

Glancing at Dalton, I wonder where he fits into this story. Surely, he's not helping a lawbreaker. He's an FBI agent. As I examine him closer I see things I've apparently overlooked—how slumped his shoulders are. How exhausted he appears. *Does he even sleep?* Now that I'm thinking about it, he's usually up before me and goes to bed after me. Then, there's the look of concern in his eyes. How they were once a shiny, bright blue, but now, dull and lifeless as if the color has been drained from them.

All this time I thought it was me causing his stress, but observing him now, I realize his concern is for Landon. All his talk about my safety and what's good for me was a mask hiding his true anxieties. It's a side of the Agent I never thought I'd see. He's always so stern, and careful about what he reveals, until this moment, which has me worried.

Why now?

What has him so troubled?

I get up off the couch and tiptoe next to him in front of the window.

Darkness has settled over the property, leaving little to see. The guards are on duty, but that isn't surprising because they never leave. There is no movement around the grounds or from inside. Again not shocking, it's usually pretty quiet at night. We haven't heard a peep from the scanner, which makes me believe Landon has switched it off at his end. That makes me consider how he's able to do that without them knowing.

"Dalton?"

"Hmmm," he mumbles while glaring out the window.

"How do you suppose Landon has radio contact without them knowing?" I cross the room to resume my post in front of the scanner.

"Well, there are several things." He pauses as he turns

around, crosses the room and sits down beside me. "Several products on the market these days." He glimpses at the silent scanner. "But, I suppose with the kind of money Landon has…" He stops talking as he glares at the scanner, obviously deep in thought.

I wait anxiously for him to finish talking, but am met with more silence. He appears completely lost in thought. Sharply, his head snaps in my direction his expression peculiar, before he springs out of his chair and hurries to his desk.

Startled by his actions, my eyes are glued to him, waiting for an explanation.

Dalton is busy pounding furiously on his laptop.

I don't want to interrupt him, but do anyway. "What are you doing?"

"Just a sec," he replies as his fingers fly across the keys.

I sit watching him quietly. He is fully concentrating on what he is doing, while I'm dying on the inside wondering what has come over him. I know it has something to do with the scanner and the radio connection we have with Landon, but I'm curious to know what that means to Dalton.

As time passes, I find myself lost in my own thoughts while I stare at the scanner, willing it to make noise. *What could he be doing? And, why is it so quiet?* Dalton's voice pulls me out of my deliberations.

I glance over at him and see his cell phone is attached to his ear as his fingers remain on the keyboard, typing furiously.

I tune into the one-sided conversation.

"Yeah," he answers and waits for a moment. "Implant," he responds and waits again. "Yeah, I'm sure there's no other possible way." His fingers stop moving. "Yeah, anything and everything." He shuts his phone, essentially ending the call, and goes back to typing on his laptop.

Fury burns through me as I'm ignored, yet again, even though it was something I've said that triggered his frenzy. He knows something, that he's not willing to share, how shocking. This is nothing new, but still irritates me. I leave him alone for a few more minutes before I'm literally going to burst.

"What the hell is going on?" I ask a little more forceful than I intended.

Dalton lets out a puff of air and finally halts his fingers.

"I'm sorry, Lexi. It's just when you mentioned the radio contact Landon is making and how it's possible, it clicked." He sits back and rubs his hand over his face.

When it looks like he isn't going to elaborate, I get mad. "And?"

"And, this may give us something to go on."

"What do you mean?"

"Well, if Landon is using what I think he's using to communicate with..." he waves his hand at me for the answer.

"Lawrence," I supply.

"Yes, Lawrence. Then he couldn't exactly get one of those devices out of a local Radio Shack." He scrubs his hand over his face again.

Over the past couple of weeks I've noticed that he rubs his hand over his face a lot when he's frustrated. A lot of his habits have become quite familiar, just as I'm sure he's picked up on a few of mine. We aren't exactly the definition of friends, but he has become someone I rely on. I hope he feels free to rely on me as well, although, he's a pretty private person who holds his worries and concerns close to his chest. I believe it's partly to protect me, which is completely ridiculous. I hope, at the very least, he's able to turn to me for emotional comfort. Though, I'm not holding my breath on that one either.

"So, where would you get one of those devices you're talking about?"

"Well, as far as I know, they're only available to people in our service."

"Like the FBI?"

"FBI, CIA, Secret Service, that sort of thing." He gazes at me with a puzzled look. "It doesn't make sense that he would have one."

"How do you know what kind of device he's using?"

"I don't, I'm assuming."

"How can we find out for sure?"

"Well, this type of device is internal." He glances at me as if I should know what that means.

"What?"

He takes a deep breath as he gets up and walks over to sit in the chair next to me.

"If he's using the device I believe he's using, the microphone would pose as a capped tooth and the listening piece would be implanted right behind your ear." He demonstrates by pressing a spot right behind my ear. "The beauty of this type of device is when you press it the whole thing turns on and off. That's how he was able to go silent tonight." He finishes, somewhat gloating, as he moves his hand back to his lap.

"Okay, but why would he want silence?" I ask, already knowing he won't have an answer. I'm just thinking out loud, which can be one of my annoying habits.

His expression turns sour as he peeks over at me.

"The good news is that if he is using the device I think he is, it can help us a great deal." He plays with the scanner, flipping through channels, completely ignoring my last question.

"Help us? How?" I'm as curious as ever.

"Well, not only can we hear him, but it also has GPS, so we'll know where he is at all times." He gives up on the scanner and returns to his desk. "That's what I've been doing over here. There are only certain places that you can get one of those devices and limited amount of places that will implant them. My guys have been going through the list to see where Landon got his and who implanted it." He begins typing on his laptop again.

I mosey to his desk and peek over his shoulder at what he is doing. "And why do we want to know that?"

"Well, that can lead us to who is helping him. We already know that he's not alone in this." He points toward the scanner. "We need to know who else is involved and how close they are to him," he sighs as he runs his hand over his face once again.

"Does it matter?" I don't really understand the relevance.

"Yes," he states as a matter of fact. "I need to know how

many people could screw this up. If we decide to do something, such as make an attempt to rescue Landon. I would really like to know who the good guys are as opposed to the bad. As much as I'd like to think that we're the only ones out here for Landon, we know there are others with a very different agenda... including Landon himself." He goes back to typing again.

I sit quietly thinking of his explanation. There are so many questions floating around my head, but I know he's not going to elaborate any further.

"You never finished your story," I blurt out, hoping he will revisit the story, because with him, it's a toss of the coin whether he will or not.

His fingers pause on the keys as he sits quietly before spinning on the chair to face me.

"No I didn't, did I?" He runs his hand over his face again while peeking over at me, his face full of resistance. "Where was I again?"

I can really notice the exhaustion after my revelation. Heck, I'm sure I resemble him in that category. Sleeping hasn't been a huge priority since our arrival. I know how little sleep I get—he gets even less. I wish I was a more compassionate person. Normally, I would tell him to go to bed early for a change, but my curiosity outweighs everything else.

"You were sitting in your office reading his file." I berate myself for encouraging him to continue when clearly his time would be better spent resting, but I know he won't rest even if I suggested it, so I forge ahead.

Dalton gets up, walks over to the couch and plops back down.

I quickly walk over and sit next to him as he leans his head back and closes his eyes.

He sighs.

CHAPTER 12

When I open my eyes, I stare at the frightened boy sitting across from me and it's clear to see he has been through hell and back. Expecting him to disclose the events of the past year—to a complete stranger, nonetheless—is wishful thinking.

Even though I'm fairly new to this position with a solid year under my belt, I know what my training would have me do in this situation, but my gut tells me something different. My training taught me to inform my superiors, to bring in a more experienced officer to deal with Landon. However, glancing at the young man before me, I decide my inexperience may be an advantage rather than a hindrance.

If only I can get him talking. *Oh, who am I kidding?* What I really want is for him to make eye contact with me. It's rather unnerving when someone refuses to make eye contact. My training would classify him as a liar. But, once again, this situation is surrounded by unknown circum-stances. From the small amount he has already revealed, he's been on the level. Now, I want to find out what happened to him.

Making the bold choice to approach this situation differently than other investigations, I decide honesty really is the best policy. I decide to share with him what I know.

"Landon?" I call out his name, still holding hope he will look at me. But, once again, he keeps his head down, so I try a little more forcefully. "Landon, would you please look at me?"

Slowly he lifts his head, but his eyes remain focused on his lap. After what feels like hours, in the silence of my office, he takes a deep breath, squares his shoulders and his eyes finally meet mine. Several emotions flicker across his features in the span of a second only to rest on a mask of indifference.

I dive in headfirst knowing that he will most likely shut down on me without notice.

"Can you tell me what happened a year ago?" I place my arms on the desk and lean closer to him in case he starts speaking. He talks so softly I'm afraid I'll miss something.

As predicted, I'm met with silence, but at least he hasn't lowered his head this time. A small victory, in my eyes.

"Landon, you've been reported missing for a year. Where have you been?" I nudge him, attempting to show concern rather than demanding information as we normally do.

The room is silent as I patiently wait for him to answer. When it seems as if I'm getting nowhere, I rethink my strategy.

"Landon, if you're in some kind of trouble..." I allow the statement to hang, waiting for any kind of reaction. For my effort, the only response from Landon is his head lowering once more.

Jesus, what happened to this guy?

"I can help you. If you just tell me what happened and where you've been for the last year, I'll work with you. Whatever it is, I can help you make it right." I plead with him to give me some kind of answer.

So softly, that I can barely hear him, he speaks. "Nobody can help me." He slowly glances up at me with the saddest eyes I've ever seen. "I just want to go home."

"How about we call your parents and let them know you're okay?" I ask, hoping to win his trust.

His eyes light up for a moment before his mask slips back into place. "Can I?"

"Of course." I push the phone on my desk toward him. "I'll get you an outside line," I pick up the handset, and dial. Completing that task, I peek at Landon's file once more and dial his parent's number before handing him the phone.

Landon leans forward, and with a trembling hand, takes the phone from me. He places it at his ear and waits. After a moment, I can tell someone answers when I see his mask completely shatter.

His voice comes out as a whisper. "Dad." Tears spring to

his eyes. He takes several deep breaths before he speaks again. "Yes, it's me."

A strong pain forms in my chest as my heart slams against my rib cage watching this helpless creature attempt to remain strong. His conversation takes a disturbing turn for the worse, when right before my eyes, Landon lets out a strangled cry and drops the phone onto the desk. He places his hands over his face and starts to sob uncontrollably.

Springing into action I grab the phone and place it to my ear.

"Who is this?"

"I'm Landon's mother." The woman reveals through tears. "Who is this?"

There is a slight shuffling noise on the other end of the phone before a deep authoritative voice comes on the line.

"Who is this? And where is my son?" The man challenges, a little more composed than Landon's mother.

"This is Agent Johnson with the FBI, and I have Landon here in my office," I answer. "Who am I speaking with?"

"I'm Landon's father. Where is my boy?" he asks, relief strong in his voice.

"He's here and he's okay. He turned up here earlier this evening wanting to go home," I explain.

"Where is here?"

"Sir, we are at my office in Italy. At the American Consulate," I add.

"Italy?" He shouts obviously surprised. "What the hell is he doing in Italy?" He is cut off by someone, I assume to be

Landon's mother, because in the next breath she is back on the line.

"Can I talk to him?" she begs me.

"Hold on a minute." I lower the phone taking a glance at Landon.

His hands are covering his face and he is still crying softly.

"Landon," I speak softly so I won't startle him.

He looks up at me with tears streaming down his face. I hold the phone out to him. "It's your mother. She would like to talk to you." He reaches out to take the phone.

He holds it for a moment before taking a deep breath and bringing it to his ear.

My mind is screaming at me to get up and leave this family to have their reunion privately, but sadly my body and heart don't quite see the situation the same way as I gaze at Landon. It's the first time I'm really seeing him. He's quite tall with his long legs tucked away under the chair. He's skinny, but not starving, more like his food has been given sparingly. I inspect his arms and hands where his long fingers are wrapped around the phone. He is wearing a suit, which in and of itself, is strange for a man of his young age.

His hand is next to his ear holding the phone in place which gives me an unobstructed view of his wrist. It's a little on the thin side, but what really grabs my attention are the red marks around it. It appears as though he may have been burned, but I can't be sure from this angle.

My eyes roam over his face, now that I have a clear view of it. He is, what most people would consider a good-looking guy. Okay… I am secure enough in my manhood to admit that Landon is gorgeous. He's the kind of guy every guy wishes they looked like and every women wishes they had. Although, his face is telling a different story tonight.

He has dark circles under his eyes as if he hasn't sleep in —well, a year. His face is pale, extremely pale, like he hasn't seen the light of day in—well, a year. His hair is longer, longer than the picture of him in the file. His eyes are a dull green, no life left in them. From his timid movements and lack of speech, my mind runs through hundreds of scenarios and circumstances that may have brought him here tonight, none of which are good.

Hearing him speak to his mother is heart wrenching. I stand to finally leave the room, giving them the privacy I should have offered at the beginning of their conversation. However, as I walk around the desk to leave, Landon speaks to me.

"They want to talk to you."

Stopping dead in my tracks at the sound of his weak voice, I turn to face him. For the first time since I've met him, his eyes meet mine without me having to ask. He holds the phone out to me and I grab it while walking back to sit down in my chair. Placing the phone to my ear, I'm dreading this conversation. Don't get me wrong, I am glad we had found Landon—alive. But, honestly, I can tell the transition back to his life will be a long and emotional road for this family.

"This is Agent Johnson," I speak into the receiver.

"When is my boy coming home?" Landon's father inquires anxiously.

"We will put him on a flight to New York in the morning," I reply automatically. "But, Mr. Miller, there are things we still need to work out." I get back to what needs to be done before we can release Landon.

"I understand Agent Johnson and I've encouraged my son to cooperate. We just want him home. The sooner, the better," he insists, showing all the signs of a professionally trained physician in the ability to remain calm under pressure.

"Thank you, Sir. We only want to help your son." My eyes meet Landon's attempting to convey the truth in my statement.

I want to help Landon above everything else because there's no doubt he needs my help. And, for the first time since he walked through the front doors of this building, I think we're all on the same page.

For the next couple of hours Landon reveals his unbelievable story. He began from before he disappeared, to the moment he walked into the Consulate. It's a story straight out of a horror movie and hard to believe it all happened. But, judging by his behavior, there's no denying it is all true.

By first light of the following morning, we have a plan in place. I have spent hours listening to Landon and conferring with my superiors. Everything is set and we are ready to do what needs to be done.

Landon and I are scheduled to be on the first plane to New York. I'm heading back to the States with him because

I feel he needs me, even if it's only for companionship. He's been through enough.

His parents are meeting us when we land and we will continue to get any information we need from Landon. I had no idea how this whole thing would blow up in my face once we reached New York.

CHAPTER 13

*D*alton has retreated into his thoughts. That much is evident as he stops talking. I place my hand on his arm and squeeze, attempting to pull him back to the here and now. His story is incredible. But, there are still things unanswered—things I wish he would reveal.

"Did he cooperate?"

Dalton looks at me stunned, almost as if he forgot I was here before he clears his throat.

"What?"

"Did Landon cooperate?"

"Uh, yeah," he mutters quietly before glancing down at his lap and running his hand over his face, clearing his thoughts, I'm certain.

I wait patiently for him to continue, and as the time ticks by, it appears as if he isn't going to reveal anything. I can't wait any longer.

"Well. What did he say? Where had he been?" I impatiently wait for the rest of the story.

"Lexi, those are answers I can't give you." He continues to scrub his hand over his face.

Can't or won't?

I am furious.

Landon's past is critical to our operation. Without knowing all the facts, how am I expected to know what to do? Does Dalton not see the importance of full disclosure while we're here putting our lives on the line dealing with the criminals next door? How can he leave me hanging like this?

"Dalton, please. You can't just leave it like that. You have to tell me what happened. Where he was and why?"

"The only thing I can tell you is that when we landed at JFK, all hell broke loose." He turns to face me. "We landed at the airport where we were greeted by Landon's parents who brought a team of lawyers with them. I don't know what happened." He grabs my hand, giving it a squeeze. "One minute we were discussing what will happen next, and out of nowhere, Landon is being dragged away by his parents, while their team of lawyers are explaining to me his rights."

"Why would they do that?" I ask, not understanding any of this.

"Exactly what I thought." He brushes some hair off his forehead. "After that, things moved very quickly. A ton of suits who work for the FBI took over everything. I was ushered back to our bureau and debriefed for hours." He runs both hands over his face, clearly agitated. "I never saw Landon or his case again. I was moved to another department and told not to discuss this case with anyone."

"So how come you came to see me? And why are you working on the Alistair case now?" I'm extremely curious of his involvement after all these years.

"I'm not."

What?

None of this makes sense. He introduced himself as an FBI agent. He acted as if he were investigating. In fact, he told me he was investigating all of them. I sit up straighter, completely puzzled.

"Lexi, this *was* my case. The one that got away. The one I never solved," he explains, as if that should mean something.

I stare at him waiting for him to continue.

"I couldn't let it go. Landon." He stops, letting out an aggravated breath. "He was the one case that haunted me all these years. I just started looking into Alistair last year, and what I found disturbed me even more. I knew I couldn't let this go until Alistair was behind bars." He leans his head back on the couch and stares up at the ceiling.

"I get it. My Dad was a cop. Remember? I've heard this story before." I glance over at him. "Can you answer one more question for me?" I ask in a quiet voice, terrified of the question or perhaps more petrified of the answer.

"What's that?" He asks turning his head to peek at me.

"Do you think Landon's a criminal?" I whisper.

Dalton's gaze holds mine for a moment before his response comes much quicker and sharper than I'd expect. "No," he says with conviction.

He turns his head to stare up at the ceiling again.

I lean my head back and close my eyes to think about everything he told me.

CHAPTER 14

*A*s my eyes snap open, I glance back as we pull out of my driveway and down the street in Haley's car. I watch my house disappear behind us even while the FBI still occupies the premises. What a weird feeling. Haley's voice pulls me from my reflection as I turn my head to give her my complete attention.

She's sporting an expectant expression, which suggests to me that I've missed whatever she said.

"I'm sorry. What were you saying?"

"I said. Where are we going?"

"Oh. Um…" I hesitate, giving it some thought. I hadn't considered beyond getting past the FBI and leaving the house. With my newly acquired freedom, any strategies for an investigation have escaped me.

"How about we start with lunch because I'm starving? Then we can figure out where to go from there," Haley suggests.

And that is why she is my best friend. She always seems

to know the right answer. "Sounds good to me," I agree as she begins to navigate the car toward a restaurant.

Still deep in thought, I hardly notice when Haley pulls her vehicle into the parking lot of a local diner we frequent. Not that it's crossed my mind in the last 24 hours, but now that we're here, I realize how famished I actually am.

As we climb out of the car and wander inside, my mind drifts to where we should start looking for information. Now that I'm free to fully explore and get answers, there are a million questions running through my brain. But, I can't think of one place to go, or even one person to talk to, who will help solve this mystery.

Haley enters the restaurant as I follow. She sits down in a booth and I slide in across from her. My movements have become shadows of hers and I need to snap out of it, but I'm having trouble doing so.

A waitress comes over, placing menus in front of us, not that either of us need them as we already know what they have to offer. She does take our drink order and promises to return in a minute.

"Do you want to know what I think?" Haley asks.

That's a given. Haley has helped me solve more problems in my life than I care to remember. Her opinion has always meant a great deal to me and always will. I'm so relieved she's here with me, but more elated that she understands.

"Yes." I lean forward resting my arms on the table giving her my undivided attention.

"I think we need to find out everything we can about

Alistair. Also, I think we need to find out everything we can about Landon." Her last statement is spoken in barely a whisper.

It's hard to tell if she's afraid someone will overhear, or, if she feels I may break down hearing his name. Which let's face it—the latter is more expected after my display last night. However, I'm not about to break down again. I've done all the crying I am going to do. Now that I have my freedom, I know what I have to do, which is to find Landon and bring him home.

I'm a little surprised Haley is helping me though. I honestly believed she would tell me to forget about Landon, and she would have every right to. I've only known the guy for a month. Surely, that isn't enough time to fall in love. I told him that I loved him. *How could I do that?* How could I stand in a room full of strangers and declare my love for a man I hardly know? *What is wrong with me?*

"Stop that right now." Haley snaps, essentially breaking my self-deprecation.

"Stop what?"

"You know what." She glares at me in challenge.

I'm not stupid. Haley knows me too well and calls me out for playing dumb. Therefore, I ask the question that has been burning in my mind since last night.

"Do you think I'm crazy?" I hope no one overhears.

"No," she simply answers.

"Why not? I mean, I hardly know the guy. Come on, Haley. If I were you, I would think I was a little crazy."

"Lexi, the heart wants what it wants, and your heart

wants Landon." She reaches across the table, taking hold of my hand, giving it a little squeeze.

"How do you know that?" I whisper, curiosity burning.

"Because, in all the time you were married to that... man... You never once looked at him like you look at Landon. You never once had a sparkle in your eye when you spoke of him. And, you never once defended him when I called him a loser or a bum." A smirk spreads across her features.

I think about her statement. We've had many conversations about my former husband, and she's right. I've never defended him to her. As for the other stuff she said, I'll just have to take her word for it because I have no idea what I look like when I talk about David, or Landon, for that matter. The only thing I know for certain is that I'm glad she's on my side and helping me through this nightmare.

The waitress strolls up to our table, putting an end to our conversation.

I order lunch, wondering if my stomach can handle eating anything. It's been churning since last night, so I order a light salad just to be on the safe side.

Apparently, Haley doesn't share my line of thinking, and orders me a bowl of soup to go along with my salad to keep up my strength, her words not mine.

Once our food arrives, we eat in silence, both lost in our own thoughts. After we finish our meal, it's back to business.

"So where do you think we should start?" I ask Haley, hoping she has come up with a plan of action.

"Well, first we need to know who that guy..." She

pauses for a moment to think. "Alistair is... We have to find out everything we can about him, and the first place we should start is..." She pauses for dramatic effect and sets her fork down on her plate. It dawns on me immediately that I won't like where she's heading with this line of thinking. "I think you should call your father," she mutters under her breath.

Something in me already knows she's going to suggest my father's involvement. In any other circumstance, she'd be dead right. My father was a police officer for many years. In fact, he was the Chief of Police. If there is anyone who can run a background check on Alistair, it is my father. On the other hand, if Alistair is as dangerous as I think he is, my father will want to know what is going on. Why I'm involved with such a dangerous man in the first place. He'll have too many questions that I can't answer. No, bringing my father into this will only cause him to worry about me needlessly. There is no way I can involve him.

My family is a subject I refuse to think about most of the time because of our complicated history. I lived with my mother most of my life and visited my father during summer vacations.

When I was at the impressionable age of fourteen, my mother married Philip Jones, a football player fifteen years her junior. Renee is not your typical mother, and decided her parental responsibility to me was done. My mother spent most of my childhood moving us from one place to another. Not that I minded at the time, it was rather adventurous. However, as the years pass by, and I never had friends for more than a couple of months at a time, life became rather lonely.

I wasn't a typical kid that went outdoors to play, joined clubs or had an abundance of hobbies. I usually stayed home cleaning, cooking or doing laundry. I did almost everything around the house. I even balanced the checkbook.

My mother is rather erratic—always changing jobs, boyfriends and cities. I spent a lot of time nursing her back from a broken heart. I love her, even though she was never a typical, traditional mother I envy others for. When she finally married Phil, I decided not to go on the road with them and moved in with my father.

My father is a whole other story. He's been a bachelor since my mother left him. If he had a girlfriend, I never knew about it. It was never a topic of discussion between the two of us. I saw him for such short periods of time, but it was enough to re-enforce how alike we are. Neither one of us were much for talking even in each other's company.

He is the complete opposite of my mother. Where Renee and I moved around a lot, my father has lived in the same house since we left him. He is a pillar of stability in my life. When I moved in with him I took over all the household duties out of habit and he never once complained.

For four years we live harmoniously with each other. He hardly ever tried to make me talk to him. In fact, he only tried when he believed something serious happened to me. I love my father, but he can be overly protective and not very understanding about certain situations. The other good thing about living with my father was that Haley lived in the same town.

There is no way I can involve my family in this situation. They will never understand what I'm trying to do. And, even though Harry's connections in the police department could help me greatly, I'll have to think of another way to learn what I need to know without my parents having any knowledge.

"Lexi? Your father…" I cut her off.

"Not on your life. There's no way he can find out any of this." I hope she'll drop the subject.

"Why not? He could help. A lot."

"I know, and in any other situation I'd agree, but not this one. No. Harry would just freak out if he knew what was going on."

She lets out a sigh. "I guess you're right," she concedes in defeat.

"Look, let's head back to your place where I have access to a computer. I'll also call my PI friend to see what he can find out," I propose, hoping to deflect the subject away from my father.

"Okay. There's also a few people I couldn't get a hold of this morning. I'd like to try again."

With a plan in place, we leave the restaurant and head to Haley's.

After placing a call to the PI, I jump on her computer. There are a few articles about Alistair's legitimate businesses, but very little of anything else.

I do learn that his home base is in Italy and it's the city from which he spends most of his time. He is a man of extreme wealth who still has half the world fooled by his business practices. I'm surprised at the amount of press he has about his legitimate businesses. *Does the business world not know who he really is?*

The most shocking piece of information is he has two brothers who are partners in his businesses. This is the first I've heard about his brothers. Although, no one has said anything to me about Alistair either.

Haley begins to make the calls to the people she wasn't able to speak to earlier. I'm not certain who she has spoken to already, or what kind of information she has found out yet.

I, on the other hand, keep looking for anything which will explain what happened last night. Sadly, after an hour of searching, I am still no closer to the truth.

Haley sits with a defeated expression on her face.

"Well, did you find out anything?" I ask.

"No," she sighs heavily. "Nobody knows anything about last night or about what happened fifteen years ago," she sighs. "Lexi?" She peers at me. "I'm not sure where we go next." She rests her elbows on her knees and rubs her temples with her fingers.

It's very unusual to see Haley so defeated. So, I immediately rush to her side. I need her now more than I ever have. Putting my arm around her shoulder, I hug her close to me.

"Stay with me." I plead. "I need you. I can't do this alone."

"Oh, Lexi." She hugs me tight. "I'm not going anywhere," she assures me as she rubs my back.

We sit holding each other.

The silence swirls around us, intensifying the tension in the room. Combined with our lack of sleep, it's difficult to remain focused on our task.

Swiftly, Haley lifts her head from my shoulder, gives her hair a toss and stands up.

"Come on," she commands as she heads for the door.

"Where are we going?" I stand to follow.

"The club." She walks out the door.

And, just like that—Haley—the strong, independent woman I've always known her to be is back.

Bewildered, I remain still for a moment, then spring up and rush out the door to catch up to her.

CHAPTER 15

By the time we arrive at the club my mind is working overtime trying to figure out what we're going to say or do.

Haley remained silent the entire drive. If she has a plan of attack, she isn't sharing it with me. I have no idea what she hopes we'll accomplish here, but if it brings us any information at all, I'm in.

As we pull down the alleyway, it surprises me to see a man at the door. I'm not sure what I expected, but I sure didn't expect the place to be open. It appears as if it's business as usual even in Landon's absence.

My heart aches at the sight.

My car door swings open, shaking me from my thoughts.

"Good afternoon, Miss Shaw," the doorman greets as he holds my door open.

"Afternoon." I force a smile on my face.

Haley is around the car to my side by the time I stand. She rushes to the entrance of the club with me bringing up the rear. She is on a mission, not even waiting for the doorman, as she rips the door open and heads inside.

Of course, I'm right on her heels.

Once inside, it's a short wait before the door to the club opens, and one of the bartenders enters the room.

"Afternoon, ladies. Miss Rose, how are you?" He fawns over Haley with a friendly smile on his face.

"Cut the crap. Where's Leroy?" she snaps.

The man's smile quivers before he composes his features once again. "Leroy is busy today. What can I help you with?"

"Nothing. You can go find Leroy and tell him I want to see him now," Haley demands.

The man turns around, heads to the office in the corner, swings open the door and stands to the side. He raises an eyebrow at us as he waves us in.

Haley walks to the door with me following along. Her greatest strength is getting people to do what she wants.

Once we enter the office, the man shuts the door trapping us in the room. I head over and sit in the chair in front of Landon's desk as Haley stands beside me.

Memories of my first time flood my mind. I think about Landon trying to warn me about this place, and about him.

I wonder where I'd be had I listened to him?

"Why are we here?" I ask, Haley.

"To get information." She shrugs one shoulder.

"They're not going to tell us anything."

"No, not outright, but if we can get in." She leans in closer to me and whispers, "Maybe we can snoop around."

"Snoop around where?" I whisper even lower.

"I'm not sure yet."

"Well." My eyes wander to the other door across the room.

"Well, what?"

"Landon has an apartment through that door." I point to the door in question.

Haley gives me a harsh glare letting me know an explanation is in order. There is so much I haven't told her, so much I kept to myself. I really am a horrible friend.

"Hey." She grabs a hold of my arm. "I told you, we're not doing that now. We have too much to worry about without adding guilt to the list." She smiles.

I nod my head as a lump forms in my throat. Why I ever thought this woman wouldn't understand is beyond me.

"But, just remember. Someday soon you will be answering my questions." Her tone leaves no room to argue.

The door to the office opens and the man of the hour waltzes in.

"Ladies," Leroy greets us as he steps around the desk to sit down.

He looks… comfortable and I become uncomfortable. He looks wrong sitting in Landon's chair at Landon's desk. This whole situation is wrong. Leroy appears calm as if nothing is happening.

"What is going on?" Haley successfully clears the room of any awkward silence.

"Miss Rose, please calm down." Leroy raises his hands in a defensive position.

"No, Leroy. Tell us what is going on? What are you doing?"

"Enough." He stands up crashing the chair he is sitting in against the wall. "That is enough. My hands are tied. There is nothing I can tell you," he says voice raised.

I need to say something to bring the tension in the room down before he throws us out of here for good.

"Leroy, please. We're all on the same side here. All I want to know is that something is being done." I'm hoping to get some kind of response from him.

"Yes-s-s!" he hisses the answer as he straightens the chair out and sits back down.

"Thank you," I respond as a thought occurs to me. "May I use the restroom please?"

He stares at me for a moment before answering. "Go ahead." He waves his hand toward Landon's apartment. "You know where it is," he sighs, surely not liking the thought of being left alone with Haley.

I get up, and walk to the apartment door, pause as I turn the handle and glance back to the two of them.

Haley eyes me before she occupies the chair I was sitting in and turns her attention to Leroy, essentially beginning her interrogation. I want to feel badly for him, but sadly, I don't.

I open the door and enter the apartment making sure to close it tight behind me. Once inside, I take a deep breath and glance around the room. It's a weird feeling being here without Landon, not knowing where he is—if he's okay. It feels wrong.

I walk briskly to the hallway knowing that all the rooms that are of interest to me are down there. I head straight to Landon's room coming to a halt in front of the door. I hesitate momentarily wondering if this is such a good idea after all. I open the door and creep in, half expecting him to appear out of thin air and start yelling at me for being here. When that doesn't happen I move to the center of the room. Spinning around slowly, I think about where to begin my search.

I spot the closet and think it's the best place to start, so I tiptoe over there. Opening the closet door it's immediately clear how organized everything is—not a thing is out of place. I already know Landon is a control freak, but seeing it firsthand is a whole other experience.

His suits are on individual hangers, suspended from rails and are spread along both sides of the closet. They go all the way to the back wall. There's an enormous amount, many more than one man needs. Several dozen pairs of shoes are neatly placed on the floor underneath. Overhead shelves run along the top of the racks on both sides of the closet.

Situated at the back wall of the closet is a five drawer dresser with a jewelry box resting on top. I swear there's a spotlight on the box.

I tiptoe over to stand in front of the dresser and stare at the box. I don't want to open it. It feels wrong. But, I feel as though I have no other choice, so I reach out, open the lid and examine its contents. Nestled inside are a row of watches, all perfectly lined, and as I think about the excessive wealth being displayed inside this box, I snap the lid shut.

I reach down and slide open the first dresser drawer. My eyes are met with underwear and socks. It's in this moment I realize the intimate view I'm getting of Landon's life. It's so wrong, but I can't seem to stop as I push the first drawer shut and open the next. Pajama bottoms. Sighing, I close that drawer and open the third, which is filled with T-shirts in neat piles, but they offer no answers, so I slide it shut and pull open the final drawer. In this drawer are several pairs of old, ripped up jeans. With a huff, I shut the drawer, knowing I'm getting nowhere fast and also running out of time.

I spin around, eyeing the shelves above his suits. On one side, the entire shelf is filled to the ceiling with sweaters, all neatly folded and stacked high. On the other side are boxes that remind me of cardboard filing boxes you would find in an office. *Why would he store files in a closet?*

I pull down the closest box and rip the lid off. Inside is a large black velvet box, which I eye wondering if I should look inside. Only for a moment. I pull it out and place the box on the floor. I snap open the lid and peer inside. There is a black collar with diamond studs encrusted along the center and covering the entire length. At the back of the collar is a golden lock with the initials LM engraved on it in beautiful script writing. I snap the lid closed, a sinking feeling pulling at my stomach when I realize the collar is for one of his former subs.

As a lump forms in my throat, I put the velvet box back in the cardboard box and dig further. I pull out a file folder and rifle through its contents. It's their contract and other forms that go with all the paperwork. The same exact paperwork I've previously filled out. I place everything back in the cardboard box and put the box back on the shelf. I don't want to know about his other subs. None of this is my business and it only saddens me to think about Landon with other women.

I move to the front of the closet and pull the first box off the shelf. Whether to torture myself or truly seeking clues, I'm not completely certain. When I lift the lid, I see another black velvet box and doubt whether I want to see its contents. My interest spikes seeing the difference between this box and the one I've already looked in. This one is more rectangle than square. I take a breath and snap it open the lid. Inside is an elegant gold chain, and once again it is encrusted with diamonds. There is a smaller version of a lock which fastens the chain. This is a beautiful necklace that no one would know its true meaning unless they were involved in this world. The difference in the jewelry has me reaching into the cardboard box and pulling out the file folder for more details.

As I open the file and review the pages, my hand begins to tremble and my world starts spinning. I am frozen, but manage to lower myself to the floor as I continue to read the paper in front of me. *How can this be? It must be a mistake? It must be a mistake?* The mantra replays itself in my mind.

Quickly, I jump up to pull another box down, rip open

the lid and extract the black velvet box. When I snap the lid open, nestled inside is another black collar with diamonds encrusted around it and a larger lock, initials and all. I clear the rest of the boxes from the shelf and find the same trinkets over and over again.

As I sit on the floor surrounded by the pile of boxes, I can feel tears prick the corners of my eyes. My mind spins as the confusion over the meaning of these collars is multiplied. I'm so lost in my own discovery that I don't hear anyone enter the room.

"Lexi?" Haley calls out. "Oh God. What happened?" She drops to the floor in front of me grabbing my wrists.

"What are you doing in here?" I hear Leroy's harsh words and peer up at him. He sighs heavily as he glances at me. "Jesus Christ," he mumbles and walks away.

"Lexi, honey. Tell me what's going on?"

"Why are they so different?" I'm aware my question won't make much sense to her, but it's the only thought in my head at the moment.

"What's so different?" she asks in a guarded manner.

"The collars, Haley." I hold up the offending black diamond-studded collar.

She stares at it for a moment, than glances back at me.

"Well, that is what a sub would wear. Landon, would have had it made." She doesn't get a chance to finish before I cut her off.

"I know that. But, why are the collars so different?" I ask frustrated by her lack of understanding.

"Well…" She thinks for a moment. "Sometimes we have different collars for different times."

Once again, I cut her off. "No, Haley. Why would his subs have different collars?" I snap, hoping to make her comprehend.

"What are you getting at? I don't understand what you're talking about."

I take a deep cleansing breath.

"Haley. All of these boxes have this type of collar in them." I hold up the black collar to show her. "But, one box had this one in it," I reach over, grab the case, snap it open and hand it to her. "Why the difference?" I ask, hoping she follows my drift now.

She handles the collars, examining both of them before studying me with sad eyes. I know instantly I won't like her answer as the lump in my throat grows.

"Lexi, these collars..." She holds up the black one. "These are pretty standard for a playroom. Although, leave it to Landon to embed them with diamonds." She grins. "I'm afraid this one..." She holds up the gold necklace. "This one here is for...," she pauses. "It's for someone special."

I swear I hear the 'prick,' under her breath.

Haley stands, glances around the room. "Are these all his former subs?" She points at all the boxes.

My face flames in embarrassment from getting caught snooping. "Yes," I reply weakly with no true excuse for my behavior. I'm here to find Landon and help him, which is no excuse to go through his personal belongings.

"Well, who was that one for? Maybe I know her?"

I nod my head in the affirmative, letting her know she

definitely knows her, but can't quite bring myself to convey who she is.

"Come on, Lexi. Tell me. Who is it?" She presses harder.

Swallowing, I glance up at her as I hold the necklace tightly. "Me."

She studies me for a moment as time stands still. She kneels back down and hugs me as I begin to sob.

Leroy picks that moment to stroll back in. I look up at him with tears streaming down my face.

Taking in the scene in front of him, he places a water bottle and a box of tissues on the floor. He stands to his full height, turns on his heels and strolls back out.

I feel completely lost and unsure of anything anymore. I know my feelings for Landon are strong. In fact, I told him I loved him, but even I wasn't certain how he felt, until this moment.

Freeing myself from Haley's embrace, I pick up the velvet box my collar was in. I pull out the small key that is in the bottom of the box. Opening the necklace, I place it around my neck, lock it with the key and straighten it out to dangle properly on my neck. With a small sigh, I place the key in my pocket. I grab the bottle of water and tissues off the floor, pull a tissue out and wipe my face. I unscrew the cap of the water bottle and take a big gulp before glancing at Haley. Her eyes have been focused on me intently, watching this whole process.

"Let's get him back," I whisper as I begin cleaning up the mess I've made.

Haley never says a word as she helps me clear away the

boxes. When I go to put the last box on the shelf, which is mine, she stops me.

"Wait," she calls in a normal voice, which in the quiet room, almost sounds like she's yelling.

I stare at Haley in confusion as she lunges past me and reaches up to pull something down from the shelf. It resembles a journal of some sort. I place the box back on the shelf and examine the book in Haley's hands.

"What is that?" I ask still gaping at it.

"I don't know." She opens the cover and we both glance inside.

The elegant script is Landon's. That much is evident.

Haley begins reading.

"Today is one of the harder ones. Memories keep popping in and out of my head more often than not. I want to forget. I want to live a normal life, but I'm not sure that's in the stars for me," she recites somberly.

This is Landon's journal. His personal thoughts. It's wrong to be reading it. I'm a journal writer and I wouldn't want people reading mine for any reason. Well, perhaps, Haley, but she already knows most of what's in there anyway. She continues to read and I realize I've tuned her out.

"Haley, stop." I reach for the journal, slamming it shut as I try to pry it out of her hands.

"What's the problem?" She releases it to me.

"This isn't right. We shouldn't be reading his private thoughts. It's just not right." I explain.

"Okay, but…" Haley reaches for the journal, yanking it out of my hands before placing it down the back of her pants. She pulls her shirt out to hang over and cover it up. "We're not leaving it here." She scowls at me. "It's coming with us." She leaves no room to argue. She steps around me and heads for the door.

I stand, fingering and fawning over my new lifeline— the gold necklace around my neck.

CHAPTER 16

As I stare at the ceiling, running my fingers over the necklace secured around my neck since that afternoon in the club, I begin to wonder if I will ever get an answer to what is happening in the castle next door. Turning my head, I stare at Dalton.

"What?" he asks without looking up at me.

"What time is it?" I inquire for the millionth time tonight.

"Two o'clock," he replies, then yawns.

"You should get some sleep."

"You should too." He turns his head my way.

"Touché." I smile.

Getting up from the couch, I hold out my hand. "Come on, we'll both get some sleep. I have a feeling tomorrow is going to be a long day." I pull him off the couch and drag him toward the bedrooms.

Once in the hallway Dalton pulls me to a halt.

"Sleep well Lexi." He draws me into a hug.

"You too, Dalton."

I give him a squeeze before stepping away and heading towards my room. Reaching my door, I spin around and look at him. "Hey, Dalton," I call out, causing him to halt halfway into his room.

"Yeah?"

"Thank you," I say in all sincerity.

"You're welcome," he replies, the trace of a smile on his lips before he disappears through the doorway.

His door shutting with finality is my cue to go to my room.

CHAPTER 17

The morning light shining through the window drenches my face. I pry one eye open, shutting it immediately. The brightness is too much, as I roll over to my other side praying for darkness. As I begin to wake, I remember where I am and what brought me here in the first place.

The next thought to cross my mind is Landon's voice and how I'll get the opportunity to hear it again at seven. I throw the blankets off, jump out of bed, grab my housecoat on the way out of the bedroom. I take off running down the hall towards the living room. I can't believe I overslept. Today, of all days, I should have been up before the sun.

As I turn the corner, I see Dalton camped out in front of the scanner already. I rush over, taking the seat next to him, and resume my position of staring at the black box in front of us. Without taking my eyes off the scanner, I speak to him in a rush.

"What time is it?" I ask.

"It's eight," he replies, far too casual for my liking.

"Why didn't you wake me?" I huff, the anger building inside of me as I turn to glare at him.

"You needed your rest." His eyes are locked on the scanner.

"That's not for you to decide." I'm offended by his incessant need to decide what is right for me. It's not his place to tell me what I need or don't need. I'm not a child.

"Look. Nothing's happened. In fact, he turned it back on, I think. Then he went to sleep." He shrugs.

"What makes you think that?" I ask, my anger completely dissipating by this discovery as I scowl at the black box.

"He's been too quiet. No movement. Nothing," he releases a breath of air like it's a relief to be sharing this information with someone.

We sit quietly, both of us lost in our own thoughts.

"What do you think went on last night?" I ask, afraid of his answer.

"I don't know." The tone of his voice suggests he knows more than he's letting on.

"Look, Dalton, I know you feel some kind of..." I pause searching for the right word. "Loyalty—towards Landon, but..."

"It's not loyalty," he sighs, as he flails his arms around. "It's my job, Lexi. You know that," he releases a breath of air as he rubs his hand over his face. "What I know about Landon's past is not my story to tell. Even if I could, I wouldn't. That's up to him." He points to the scanner. "I'm not trying to be difficult. I'm not trying to intentionally keep things from you, but you have to understand…" He studies me with the saddest eyes I've ever seen. "What happened to Landon fifteen years ago is not easily explained." He stops and rubs his temples. "I wouldn't want anyone to talk about it without my permission," he sighs.

It's easy for me to come up with scenarios for what happened to Landon. As my mind runs wild with several unbelievable tales, I try hard not to jump to conclusions. It's becoming increasingly difficult to stop my mind from going in those directions.

In the first couple of days of being here, I refuse to even think about his missing year. However, the closer I get to him, the stronger my need to know becomes. Not knowing what I'm up against, not knowing who these people are and what they are capable of is draining.

There are things that are obvious. Things, that unless I'm truly naive while walking around with blinders on, a person can't help but notice. The FBI's involvement, for one thing, because a petty thief or small-time criminal would not garner the attention of the Bureau. There is also the team of players from Landon's nightclub. No way those people are just bartenders or managers as they've been portrayed. Even I noticed that my first visit. But, who they are and what they're really up to has eluded me so far. Landon's pool of people are tight and none of them are willing to share information.

I did have what I thought was a special relationship

with Landon's father which I hoped would produce some sort of information. It took me three days to work up the courage to contact him, again. After many phone unanswered calls, I became determined to see him in person. That is what led me to showing up unannounced at his front door.

CHAPTER 18

*A*dvancing along the driveway affords me an exceptional view of the massive property surrounding the estate. This spread would most certainly be referred to as an estate.

I pull my vehicle around to the front doors, throw the gear shift into park as I stare out the windshield in astonishment. If I were here under ordinary circumstances, I would admire everything. However, since I'm here on a mission, my admiration will have to take a backseat. That doesn't mean I'm completely ignorant to the immense wealth on display here.

Exiting my vehicle, I make my way to the front doors. And, yes, there are two huge wooden doors to this mansion. I ring the doorbell, knowing I'm expected after my encounter at the front gate. At first I thought I may have a problem when I saw the gate, but there was a speaker box planted right at my window as I pulled up. A minute or so later a voice came through the speaker asking who I was and what my purpose for being there was. Once I explained, the gates opened and enabled me to enter.

As the front door swings open, I emit a loud gulp.

"May I help you?" a woman, whom I assume is a maid because she's wearing a uniform, speaks sharply. All business no pleasantries—implying I'm disturbing her and verifying that she was not the one who I spoke to at the gate.

"I'm here to see Dr. Miller." I attempt to sound like an invited guest.

"Please, come in." She moves to one side opening the door wider as she motions inside.

I walk a few steps past her into a grand entrance, pausing once I'm in.

It's evident from the mansion's exterior how grand the place is, but nothing prepares me for its elegance and opulence. And, I'm only in the foyer, which happens to be longer than the entire length of my house. I'm clearly out of my element.

I mean—my ex-husband and I are not poor, by any stretch. But, this place is something I've only ever seen in the movies.

Places like this just don't exist in real life, or so I thought.

As I stand waiting for my next set of instructions, my eyes scan the room, taking in the fine marble floor and two grand staircases on either side of the room, leading to the second level. There are huge art pieces on each wall leading up the staircases that appear old and expensive.

Between the two staircases sits a round table with the biggest floral arrangement I've ever seen perched on top.

The walls are painted a warm beige color. Not your regular house paint you purchase by the gallon from a home improvement store. No siree. This paint has texture to it adding to the ambience of the artwork. I know Landon's mother is an interior designer, but I had no idea how good she truly is, or how rich Landon's family really is.

I'm lost in the enormity of the house, so out of my league. My nerves are on edge, making me reconsider imposing on this family in their most vulnerable time.

The maid snaps me out of my reverie.

"Please, follow me," she commands as she strides away.

I follow dutifully behind her, attempting to survey everything along the way. We pass by the table with the floral arrangement positioned so aesthetically. I just know they're replaced daily.

Proceeding under the staircase and to the right, we head down a hallway where the walls are lined with pictures of whom I assume are Landon's family. Both sides of the walls are covered from floor to ceiling with pictures. Slackening my pace, I try to catch a glimpse of as many as I can.

This family represents the epitome of happiness. In every photo, people are smiling or laughing. My stomach flip-flops knowing that despite everything in this house appearing picture perfect, it's the furthest from the truth. Even though I have never met Landon's mother, my heart aches for her and the grief she must be feeling.

The maid stops in front of a large doorway, turning around to address me.

"Please, have a seat in the sitting room. Dr. Miller, will be right with you." She gestures for me to enter the room.

I tiptoe past her, muttering my thanks as I pass the doorway and enter the large room. My surroundings go unnoticed as butterflies swarm my stomach, intensifying my nervousness by causing my hands to tremble.

Instantly, I sit on the sofa holding my hands tightly in my lap in an attempt to stop them from shaking. I have no idea what I'm going to say, or what I'll ask Dr. Miller without offending him. But I'm hoping, at the very least, he'll share what is happening to Landon. That is my desire, but the reality is—even after my brief meeting with Dr. Miller—they really have no idea who I am or what interest I have in their son, leaving me at a disadvantage. I Hope the sincerity of my intent is evident, that they'll be forth-coming in sharing information with me.

A few minutes pass before Dr. Miller and a woman, whom I can only assume is his wife, enter the room. They sit on the loveseat across from where I'm sitting. Mrs. Miller grabs her husband's hand, holding on as if he's her lifeline. She is a beautiful woman with auburn-colored hair and sharp green eyes. It's easy to see where Landon gets his looks, as he's definitely a mixture of the two people seated across from me. Mr. Miller's hair is streaked grey, but against his blond hair, it's hardly noticeable. Mrs. Miller, on the other hand, has flecks of silver peeking out of her roots at the front of her hairline, permitting me to deduce that she's recently missed a hair appointment. Women of her stature don't let their roots grow in, at least, that's what Haley's mom always used to say.

My heart aches a little more as I glance at her face. She doesn't give anything away, but it's evident she has a mask in place for my benefit. I'm not sure what they're hiding or why, but I'm determined to find out anything and everything they're willing to share.

As we sit in silence, I steady my nerves, searching for the determination I had when I reached the decision to bother these people. Not one word is spoken as I realize they are waiting for me to start this conversation. But suddenly, my mouth goes dry rendering me speechless. I agonize over how this conversation will go, and if I really want to trouble them. Gathering the courage needed, I decide to start at the beginning.

"Dr. Miller, Mrs. Miller, I'm sorry for barging in on you in your time of…" I stop, fully comprehending I have no idea what the extent of the situation is, which leaves me at a loss for words.

Is Landon kidnapped? Is he being held against his will?

From my point of view, Landon left my house a willing participant. There was no struggle, fight or even an attempt to get away from Alistair. So honestly, what are my concerns?

I know, without a shadow of a doubt, that Landon is in some kind of trouble. Although, it appears he left of his own free will. I know it's not true.

"Alexandria," Dr. Miller, speaks in an even voice. "What are you doing here?" He tries to sound surprised by my visit, but fails miserably.

"Dr. Miller, I need to know." I stare only at him. "What is happening with Landon?" My voice sounds more confident than I feel.

I hear Mrs. Miller's sharp intake of breath before she bows her head, hiding her face from view.

Dr. Miller fares better as he makes eye contact with me while considering my question.

"Alexandria," he sighs before I cut him off.

"It's Lexi, Dr. Miller." I'm hoping the familiarity will make him see I'm more than some curious onlooker.

He lets out a ragged breath of air, steeling himself before continuing. "Lexi, I don't know what you know, but…" I cut him off once again.

"I know nothing. That's why I'm here. Please, Dr. Miller."

Mrs. Miller snaps her head up in surprise at the earnestness of my voice. Our eyes meet and I implore her to understand my position. I'm not sure she knows about me at this juncture, or if she's aware of what her son did to me. At this time, none of that matters. Under ordinary circumstances I'd be reluctant, but for now, all I care about is finding Landon.

Dr. Miller looks upon me with sympathetic eyes. I swear I've won him over, and he's going to give me the information I came here to get. However, as quickly as his compassion appears, it's gone and his facial features assume a mask of indifference.

"I'm sorry you've come all this way, Lexi. But, there's nothing I can tell you." He wraps his arm around his wife's shoulders.

My temper flares. "Can't tell me, or won't?" I snap without forethought.

Dr. Miller jumps to his feet as he spits out his next words. "Do not speak to me in that manner. In my home. In front of my wife," his voice is full of venom and his breathing becomes labored.

Mrs. Miller recoils from her husband's outburst.

I glare at Dr. Miller, stunned by the thunder in his roar. At this moment, he reminds me of Landon—of that fateful night in his club—and I'm afraid, hurt. The expression on my face must clearly display my feelings because he shakes his head and runs his hands through his hair, taking a calming deep breath before sinking back into the seat beside his wife.

"Look, Lexi. I'm sorry for my…" And, once again I don't let him finish.

"Dr. Miller, I know this is a stressful time for you both." I peek at Mrs. Miller. "And, believe me when I say that I'm not here to cause you any more pain or grief. But, Landon has become… Well, I'd just like to know that something is being done. That he isn't on his own out there and that people here are trying to help him." My voice wavers and I seriously wonder if my words are having any effect.

"Lexi, everything that can be done, is being done. Trust me when I tell you that I have all of my resources working on this. We will stop at nothing to bring Landon home," he reveals in a more civilized manner, but I still have so many unanswered questions.

"Dr. Miller, where is he? And how much trouble is he in?" The questions tumble from my lips.

"That is information I'm unable to tell you." He stands from the loveseat once more.

I glance over at Mrs. Miller, who is staring at me with empathetic eyes trying to assess who I am and what I mean to Landon. Giving her the best helpless look I can muster, I'm hoping to appeal to her nurturing side. She lowers her head, once again, successfully hiding her face from view.

"I am sorry, but we are very busy," Dr. Miller states in a cordial, but firm tone, essentially dismissing me.

I get up from the couch and head for the door, but before exiting into the hallway, I turn around and attempt one final appeal. "You don't know who I am, but I care for your son deeply and will do everything in my power to make certain he is okay." Tears spring to my eyes.

Spinning on my heels I make my way out of the room back down the hall and out the front door.

Striding quickly to my car, I collapse in the drivers' seat as the floodgates open and the tears flow freely. Hot streams run down my face as my hands grip the steering wheel and I press my forehead against them. Grief washes over me as I think about all the anguish this poor family is going through. The expression on Mrs. Miller's face conveys all the pain and agony she is going through, and it makes my stomach twist in agony.

Even though no information was acquired, I know there is more to this story than anyone is willing to admit. Whatever happened at my house is directly related to Landon's disappearance fifteen years ago. Now, more than ever, I'm bound and determined to find answers.

A knock on my window yanks me from my breakdown.

Blinking through tears I look out, wondering if the Miller's security team is here to escort me from the premises. Shock courses through me, but quickly changes to sympathy as I come face to face with Mrs. Miller.

I put the key in the ignition and push the button to roll down my window, curious as to what has brought her.

"We don't know each other, and I'm risking a lot by being out here right now. Lexi, I believe you when you said you care for my son. In fact, I can see that you more than care for him." She steps closer to the car, running her thumb under my eye wiping the tears away. "I just want to tell you that we are doing, and will continue to do everything in our power, to make sure Landon comes home safely." She removes her hand from my face and takes a step back.

"Can you tell me where he is?"

"Italy. But, that's all I can say," she whispers as she takes another step back.

"Can you tell me anything else?"

"Please, take care. I hope we meet again." She turns and walks away.

"Thank you," I whisper, hoping she can still hear me.

I watch as she disappears into the house, wondering why she came to me in the first place. She told me where he is and they are definitely trying to help him.

What is he doing in Italy?

That explains why their house isn't frantic with a search underway. It also explains their calm behavior. They know where he is, but it doesn't appear they know what he's doing. His mother may not know the lifestyle Landon lives, but Dr. Miller sure does. He has seen firsthand what can happen when things go wrong. It seems to me that Dr. Miller appears more concerned with Landon's welfare than where he is.

Putting the key in the ignition, I start the car and cruise along the lengthy driveway, moving further away from the house. As I drive through the gate at the end of the driveway, I take one last glance at the house in the rear-view mirror. The property is picturesque and no one will ever know the anguish and pain that is taking place behind those walls.

CHAPTER 19

*I*nstead of sitting in my chair staring at the little black scanner, I find myself standing in front of the window staring out at the walls of the beautiful castle that has become my focal point since arriving in Italy. As I recall the Millers' home appears as the picture-perfect family home, I glower at the castle across from me which gives the same vibe.

Admiring the beautiful landscape and architecture of the estate, it's hard not feel envious of the proprietor. But I know, hidden behind the stone walls of that dwelling, lurks an evil entity.

A rustling noise coming from the scanner grabs my attention, and I rush back to the chair I don't remember standing up from. Resuming my position next to Dalton all of my attention is focused on the scanner that is producing slightly muffled noises.

Landon must be awake and moving around the room, but none of the sounds indicate what he is doing. I glance at Dalton, hoping he can shed some light on what's happening.

He offers a supportive gaze.

"I'm sorry," I whisper.

"I know."

Bless his soul.

"I didn't mean to accuse you of anything." I let out the breath of air I didn't realize I was holding.

"Lexi, it's all right."

He turns his head back to the scanner.

"No. It's not all right, Dalton." I place my elbows on the table in front of me, laying my head in my hands. "It's not right to treat you that way, when you're the only one who's been helping me."

A tear leaks out of my eye.

Dalton gently rubs his hand up and down my back. "I know the kind of stress you've been under. I know how difficult all of this has been for you."

"That's no excuse." I peek over at him looking him in the eye.

"No, it's not, but I understand. Besides I can take it." A playful grin spreads across his face. "And, I'm not the only one who's helped you." He turns back to the scanner.

That comment stops all playfulness immediately.

"I know, and I have every intention of making it up to her as soon as we're home."

With my attention absorbed by the scanner, guilt washes over me as I'm flooded by the memories of Haley and how poorly I treated her before coming to Italy. She stood by me throughout this entire ordeal, and in the end, I threw it all back in her face. I cut off all contact, essentially shutting her out of my life. When we return to the States, I will make things right with her. I have to. As soon as I have Landon safe at home that will be my number one priority. Haley's too important to me and I'll do everything in my power to make amends. We had the biggest argument we've ever had before I left the States, but I know in my heart she will accept my apology when offered.

My mind twists through the memories of how we ended up here—not speaking to each other. I close my eyes, thinking back on that dreadful day, and wonder how I could actually ruin the most important friendship in my life.

CHAPTER 20

*A*s I arrive home from my visit with Landon's parents—a colossal failure. I find Haley waiting for me—not a surprise at all.

I break down, while explaining to her what happened and how much of a waste of my time it turned out to be. She's quick to remind me that Landon's mother reached out to me, but it was only to reveal his location. Information that is no help at all.

To Haley, that action means a lot, even more than I realize.

"Okay, enough is enough," Haley announces, as she stands up from the couch. "No more crying. We have things to do." She starts to walk in the direction of my bedroom. "Let's go," she calls over her shoulder.

I get up and follow her to my bedroom. Haley sits casually on the bed. I'm curious to know what is running through her mind. But, as she reveals nothing, I frown, then walk into the bathroom.

Glancing in the mirror, I hardly recognize myself. I look like I've aged ten years in the short time I've been involved in this whole situation. *Whatever this situation is?* I suppose it all started when I met Landon.

Thinking back to the first night we met, he was mysterious, domineering and ridiculously handsome. I'm still astonished how quickly I fell for him. Even though he did everything in his power to push me away, he never even hinted to me the feeling was mutual. It's hard to imagine what made me stay or try to make something out of nothing. But, I did stay and try to get close to him.

Shaking my head, I get back to the task at hand. Getting ready. But, for what? I have no idea. However, if Haley says she has a plan it's definitely better than the one I've come up with on my own, so I'm ready to hear her out.

Strolling back into my bedroom, Haley is still sitting casually on my bed flipping through a magazine. She halts the pages of the magazine as she glances up at me.

"It's about time." She jumps up dropping the magazine onto the bed. "Let's go." She marches across the room and out the bedroom door.

"All right. I'm coming." I grab a sweater off the back of the chair at my vanity table and rush out the door after her.

Settling myself into the passenger seat of Haley's car, my curiosity is getting the better of me. "Where are we going?" I peer out the window watching my driveway disappear.

"Well, we've checked out his club, which was a bust."

I interject as a thought occurs to me.

"Haley? What did you do with Landon's journal?"

I had every intention of getting it from her when we left the club, but clearly I had other thoughts plaguing me that day and it slipped my mind.

"I put it in the bottom drawer of your nightstand when we got back to your house."

I scowl at her.

"No. I didn't read it, Lexi." She rolls her eyes obnoxiously as if offended.

"I knew you wouldn't." I truly do believe her.

Haley prefers to be in the loop on most things, a snoop she is not. Unless, of course, it's warranted, as with the situation we find ourselves in now, but still I can't imagine her doing something that horrendous.

"You're lying." She laughs, while gazing out the windshield watching the road ahead of us. "You thought I read it. Didn't you?" She laughs harder.

"No." I'm astonished by her accusation but laugh along with her. "No. I really didn't think you would do that. At least, not without consulting me first." I peek over at my best friend as her laughter dies down. She is genuinely a magnificent friend causing me to feel less than worthy of her friendship.

She stops the car at a red light, her laughter comes to a halt, as she turns her head and glances at me.

"You're right. I would never do something like that without consulting your first." She smiles, then turns her attention back to the road as the light turns green. She steps on the gas, moving the car forward. "But, the temptation was hard to resist. That's why I left it inside your nightstand." She peeks over at me waiting for my reaction.

I spent a few moments glaring at her just to torture her before I burst out laughing again. She joins me in laughter to the degree she almost has to pull the car over. After several minutes and numerous tears later we have ourselves under control. As I look in the mirror on the back of the visor, I wipe away the tear and mascara from underneath my eyes, and ask the question that's been on hold during this ride.

"Where are we going?"

"Don't get upset, okay?" Haley counters.

Instantly, my feathers are ruffled because the last time she asked me not to get upset we ended up at a whips-and-chains club. I imagine that's the worst it can get. *Or is it?* I look over at her to find she is concentrating a little too hard on the road for my liking. Looking out the window at the streets as they pass I try to find anything that looks familiar but there's nothing.

Until…

Haley turns down a street that is very familiar. I'm dumbfounded as I stare out the windshield and the car comes closer to the last place I ever expected to be.

"Are you kidding me?" I blurt out, all humor extinguished as Haley steers the car to the curb and comes to a halt.

"No," she shrugs.

I glower out the passenger side window, stunned she would bring me here.

The house is surrounded by a giant concrete wall blocking any view. However, I know where we are.

I search out the front windshield, then out the rear of

the car at the quiet street around us. "Why would you bring me here?" I stare daggers at Haley who only has eyes for the huge, wrought iron gate looming prominently in the driveway to keep people from entering the property unannounced. "What were you thinking?"

Haley ignores me as she checks out the street of the quiet neighborhood. At last, her gaze turns my way. "Because he lives here, Lexi?" she deadpans, as if I'm foolish for not thinking of it first.

She grabs the door handle ready to get out.

I grab a hold of her arm, pinning her in place. "We can't go in there," I state the obvious.

"Why not?" She narrows her eyes at me.

"Because we haven't been invited. Because he's not here. Because we don't even know if there's anyone here. That's why not."

"Like that's stopped me before." Haley tugs on the door handle opening the door wide and stepping out of the car.

I sit back frowning at her as she walks around the front of the car and over to the grassy knoll along the huge concrete wall. "Are you coming?" She calls to me, over her shoulder, as she halts her movement and stares up at the top.

I remain in the car for as long as I can before curiosity —as always—gets the best of me. I snap open my seatbelt, yank the door handle and step out of the car, while surveying the neighborhood. All is quiet and no one is around. I'm sure they're all working to pay for these mansions—not that there are too many houses on this street. In fact, there are only two other houses visible from here that are quite a distance away from Landon's house.

My attention returns to Haley who is still staring up at the wall with a quizzical expression on her face. Walking over, I stand next to her and follow her gaze to the top of the wall. It stands at least six feet tall.

"What are you thinking?" I shield my eyes from the glare of the sun.

"Trying to figure out how we're going to get over it," she announces.

I skim her features waiting for the humor in her statement to present itself. None does. Her face is full of concentration and determination.

"What?" I turn my whole body to her. "Are you crazy?"

"No." She sizes me up. "But, we have to get in somehow."

"Not like this." I wave my hand at the wall.

"Well, how else are we going to get in?" she says so casually it's hard to believe she's talking about committing a crime.

The thought of us getting arrested, being dragged off to jail and me having to call my father to bail us out crosses my mind. I shake my head and start back for the car. She's lost it.

"Where are you going?" Haley calls out.

"Just get in the car, Haley." I open the car door and fold myself back onto the seat, slamming the door shut, as I watch Haley out the window.

Haley takes one last look at the wall before making her way back to the car, returning to the driver's seat. I scrutinize her the entire time, surprised on the one hand that she suggested this, and not surprised, on the other hand that she suggested this.

She starts the engine before turning to me expectantly.

"Drive to the gate." I wave my hand dismissively towards the front gate.

Haley throws the car into drive, pulls in the driveway and up to the gate stopping when the intercom is aligned with her window. She rolls down the window and presses the button.

A familiar voice comes over the speaker.

"Can I help you?"

"Mrs. Howard?" I ask to be certain it's her. Although, there is no reason to question it because she has the same motherly voice she did when I stayed here on that last unfortunate occasion.

"Yes," she replies cautiously.

"It's Lexi, Mrs. Howard."

"Oh Lexi, dear. Come on up." She sounds relieved.

The gates in front of us swing open.

"Well, that was another way to go." Haley steps on the gas, moving the car up the driveway.

I smile attempting to hold back my laughter as we slowly make our way. Once the house comes into view my amusement is long forgotten as a lump forms in my throat.

Haley halts the car in front of the house.

One look at the front door reveals Mrs. Howard standing in the open doorway waiting to greet us. Still the same plump, friendly warm woman I remember.

The lump in my throat grows bigger as my hand

suddenly being squeezed distracts me from the sight at the door.

Haley gives my hand another jolt. "It's going to be okay. Remember why we're here," she reminds me before tugging on the handle and opening her door.

I watch as she gets out and begins making her way around the car. I jerk the handle, open the door and step out just as Haley makes it to my side. Together, we head toward Mrs. Howard.

"Ms. Lexi, how are you?" Mrs. Howard reaches for my hands giving them a reassuring squeeze.

"Not well, Mrs. Howard." I respond truthfully.

She pats my hand, while giving me a sympathetic look. "I know, dear," she affirms. "Well, come inside." She moves aside, allowing us to enter the house.

Being here again without Landon is extremely difficult. I'm on the verge of tears, but hold them back as we move through the house to the kitchen.

"Have a seat." Mrs. Howard waves us toward the kitchen table while she goes to the stove, pulling the kettle off of it and heads to the sink. She turns on the water, fills the pot before traipsing back to the stove.

"Can I offer you some tea?" She backtracks, appearing embarrassed for making the assumption in the first place.

"Yes, please." I put her out of her misery.

"That would be great," Haley replies too.

"Wonderful." Mrs. Howard returns to her tea-making ritual.

We sit watching her as she moves around the kitchen gathering teacups and saucers, milk and sugar servers, a tray to place everything on—and of course—a teapot with a couple of teabags dropped in it.

The kettle whistle sounds extremely loud in the silence of the room. Mrs. Howard grabs a potholder, then lifts the kettle off of the burner, pouring hot water into the tea pot on the tray. She puts the kettle back on the stove, picks up the tray and makes her way to the kitchen table.

After doling out teacups to us both and settling one in front of herself, she begins pouring tea in each cup. She sits down and begins preparing her tea. Haley and I follow suit mixing milk and sugar into our own cups. The only sound in the room is the clinking of the spoons on our cups.

When we are all settled and sipping our tea Mrs. Howard peers at me. "To what do I owe the pleasure of your visit, dear?"

"I'm here for Landon, Mrs. Howard." I give an exaggerated sigh.

"Well, he's not here today," she professes as she turns to look at Haley.

"Mrs. Howard, this is my best friend Haley Rose. Haley, this is Landon's second mother." I introduce them receiving an odd glare from Mrs. Howard but there is a small sparkle in her eye too.

"Pleasure to meet you dear." She smiles at Haley.

"Pleasure's all mine," Haley reciprocates, earning herself a slight giggle from Mrs. Howard.

Haley smiles at her, then turns and stares icily at me.

"I know Landon's not here, Mrs. Howard."

"Oh. Well, if you know, what brings you here?" Her eyes bore into mine.

"I know he's missing," I blatantly blurt out.

"Oh."

The room goes silent once more.

Mrs. Howard suddenly finds her tea more interesting than us.

Haley tips her head to the side, encouraging me to talk, to say something, but nothing comes to mind. I can feel the anguish rolling off the older woman sitting next to me. The woman who thinks of Landon as a son. *What can I say? What do you say to someone who is obviously in pain?*

"Mrs. Howard, do you know anything?" I decide being straightforward is my best bet.

"No," she answers sharply.

I can't tell if she's being truthful because she has a really good poker face. I glance over at Haley to gage her reaction. She shrugs. That's not a good sign.

"Is there anything you can tell me that will help me find him?" I look directly at her, hoping she'll look at me, but so far her tea is holding her attention.

After a few long minutes I almost give up. Almost.

"Mrs. Howard, please." I try to think of something convincing to say to her. Instead, all I can do is plead. "Please, help me bring him home."

My emotional outburst appears to be cracking through her strong exterior as she lifts her eyes to meet mine.

"Please." I present my saddest face and would get down on my knees if I thought it would help.

"There's nothing I can tell you, Ms. Lexi." She offers and I immediately deflate. "Mr. Miller is a very private person, as you know." My shoulders slump as I begin to lower my head. "But..." My eyes snap back to hers. "I'm in desperate need of running some errands and could use a ride to the store." She looks sharply at Haley then back at me.

I glance at Haley who is shaking her head vehemently, indicating a big 'No'. My eyes appeal to her for this huge favor. She surrenders with an exaggerated roll of her eyes and I know I've won her over.

"I could take you, Mrs. Howard," Haley offers.

"That would be wonderful, dear." Mrs. Howard gets up and begins clearing the table.

Haley and I have a telepathic conversation about how I owe her big time for this grand gesture.

"Mrs. Howard, why don't you let me take care of the cleanup so you two can head out." I stand, gathering our teacups and utensils from the table bringing them to the sink.

"Okay, let's hit it, Mrs. Howard." Haley also stands making a beeline to the door in the kitchen.

"I'll just grab my stuff and meet you at the car, dear." Mrs. Howard heads down a small hallway to the back of the house.

Haley steps back into the kitchen pinning me with a menacing stare. "You owe me huge."

"I know. Thank you, Haley." My eyes never flinch once. "You know she wouldn't have let us both wander through this house."

"Yeah, I know." She smiles. "Well, I better go." She turns and walks toward the door and out of the kitchen as she calls over her shoulder. "I have an old woman to take shopping."

"Haley!"

She spins around before heading out of sight.

"What?" she asks, face dead serious.

I narrow my eyes at her.

"Relax, Lexi. I'm only joking," she giggles. "I do have a grandmother and know how to treat old people." She winks walking out the door and disappearing from view.

"Haley." I yell out to her, but she just laughs harder and ignores me.

I go right to work busying myself cleaning the mess from our afternoon tea. Once everything is washed and put away I stand at the kitchen island wondering where to start. The last time I was here Landon didn't offer me a tour, so I have no idea where to begin.

I wander out of the kitchen, through the living room to another opening that leads to a long hallway. I glance down and notice several doors—some open, the others closed. I walk slowly down the hall half expecting Landon or someone else to jump out at me.

Reaching the first door, I peek in pleasantly surprised by my discovery. The room is wall-to-wall bookshelves, floor-to-ceiling tall and every shelf is full of books. The room is enormous. I glide to the center of the room and spin around slowly. It's a personal library. A readers dream. I'm in love.

I sigh, wanting desperately to explore, however that's not going to happen. Scanning the room again, I behold thousands of books that I want to run my fingers over. There's a fireplace on one wall with a Persian rug and two very comfortable looking wingback, red leather chairs. I can easily picture myself spending days on end in this room.

I reluctantly start toward the door with a feeling of longing, but with the knowledge that spending one more minute in this room I'd never leave. Reaching the doorway, I spin around to take one last glimpse at the room saying a little prayer asking to return one day and fully explore the entire room. That is my wish.

Walking out of the room, I notice another door across the hall that's closed and make my way over to it. Standing in front of it with an overwhelming feeling of trepidation, I take a deep breath and turn the handle. I push it open a crack, just enough to peek in. Relief floods me as I realize it's an office.

I open the door wider and step over the threshold. Surprisingly, it's on the smaller side—well, small for Landon Miller. There is a beautiful wooden desk that is definitely handcrafted. A big, black leather computer chair rests comfortably behind the desk. Directly behind the desk are two oversized windows revealing a picture-perfect view of the grounds outside. As I stand in the middle of the room, staring at the desk, I know I should rummage through drawers for any clues as to Landon's whereabouts or what has befallen him. But, I hesitate. Once I cross this line there's no turning back. Should I delve into his personal belongings, only God knows what will be revealed. So I hesitate.

"You can do this. It's necessary to find him," I whisper to myself attempting to relieve my mind of the guilt that's consuming me.

Striding over to the desk, I use both hands to pull the chair back—it's that heavy. I take a seat, peering at the top of the desk. Everything is in its place. A leather-bound appointment book is resting in the center, along with an expensive pen in its holder in front of the book. A computer monitor sits on the right side of the desk which has me glancing around in search of a keyboard and mouse, but find nothing.

Glancing down at the desk in front of me, there are sets of drawers on each side, plus another skinny drawer at the top in the middle. I reach out pulling open the middle drawer first. Voila! A keyboard and mouse. Now all I have to find is the hard drive.

Opening the top drawer on the left-hand side, I spot a pile of journals stacked on top of each other. I reach in and grab the first one out, placing it on the desk in front of me. I stare at it for a minute, debating over the necessity of the act I'm about to commit. The journal is more than likely filled with Landon's personal thoughts. *Should I really be reading them?*

Taking a big breath, I snap the cover open, sighing in relief as a gust of air releases from my lungs—it's blank. Flipping to the next page, I see it's blank too.

I quickly place the book back in the drawer and slam it shut.

Opening the next two drawers I find nothing useful in them either. Moving onto the right side drawers, I begin with the top one, which quickly reveals the hard drive that goes with the monitor, keyboard and mouse. I push the power button and listen as it whistles to life. The monitor turns on, the keyboard lights up and I wait for the unit to boot up. A few seconds later I'm staring at the start up screen asking for a password.

Propping my elbows on the desk, I rub my temples with my fingers, disappointed—but not really surprised Landon would have a password on his computer. I hit the power button to shut it down because there is no way I'll figure out what the password is. Shutting that drawer, I move onto the next one, sliding it open and peering inside. Frustrated once again, and feeling as if this search is hopeless I slam the drawer shut.

Faced with the last drawer, I open it and check inside. Taking up most of the space in the drawer is a wooden box. I reach in, pick it up and place it in my lap. It's an old cigar box with an exquisite carving on the top of it. I lift the lid and search inside. Nestled at the bottom of the box is a black velvet sack whose drawstring secures its contents from exposure.

Lifting it out of the box, I tug on the drawstring to open the sack and peek inside, but can't get a clear view of its contents. Reaching in, I feel a metal object and pull it out. It's a custom-made skeleton key. It's quite exquisite. I turn it around inspecting it closer wondering what it could possibly be used for. Since it doesn't help me in the least, I drop it back in the sack, pull the drawstring taut, and tuck the pouch back in the box before putting the box back in the drawer.

My search is going nowhere fast as I sit back in Landon's chair and ask for his help.

"Please tell me what I'm looking for," I whisper.

Making certain everything is back in its place, I get up from the chair, push it back under the desk and make my way around the room. There is a wooden bookcase with glass doors situated on the opposite wall of the desk. I creep over to stand in front of her and glimpse inside. The books on these shelves are old—really old. Being the book lover I am, I want to throw open the door and run my fingers along the spines, but I can't. I can't even bring myself to open the door. I'm here uninvited and it feels wrong to snoop for my own personal pleasure.

Without anything further to investigate in this room, I leave, closing the door behind me. Glancing further down the hall, I notice one last door and head in that direction. Turning the handle and opening it I peek in, and notice the washer and dryer. Disappointed, I close it knowing I won't find anything useful in there. I head back down the hallway to the living room area.

This is becoming more difficult than I could have imagined not knowing what it is I'm looking for. If only there were some hint, a little something to let me know I'm on the right track. Being in the dark about this whole situation is starting to grate on my nerves.

I move toward the staircase and make my way up slowly.

Walking around someone's house without their explicit knowledge leaves me with a creepy feeling. I feel like a peeping Tom. I have no idea how people do this all the time. There is no way becoming a burglar will be a future career choice of mine. I have absolutely no adrenaline rush to speak of. No thrill, or whatever it is criminals tend to say they feel when committing a crime. It just feels wrong. I feel like a snake slithering around Landon's house without his permission—bottom line.

Reaching the landing upstairs, I tiptoe down the hallway still half expecting someone to jump out and say 'caught you.' There are eight rooms on this level if memory serves me correctly. Two of those doors I have prior knowledge of, one being Landon's bedroom and the other his submissive chamber. The other six are complete mysteries to me as I make my way toward the first door on the right. I swing the door open and peek inside—a bathroom. I shut the door quickly and move on.

After discovering five guest bedrooms, I've almost given up hope when I hear voices coming from the bottom of the stairwell.

"We're back," Haley calls out breaking the silence of the house, and quite frankly, causing me to jump and grab my heart.

It's not bad enough I'm on edge wandering around this huge house on my own, but did she really feel it necessary to scare the crap out of me too? "I'm up here." I reach the last door left unexplored.

I hear Haley trudging her way up the staircase and I'm glad I hear only her footsteps which lets me know Mrs. Howard is not with her.

I reach for the door handle and try to turn it but I'm met with resistance. It's locked. Damn it.

"I will never forgive you for what you just made me do," Haley exclaims, her tone a little more than a whisper. She strides down the hall glaring daggers at me as if I just ordered her off to war on a bloody battlefield.

"Really, Haley? You took a woman to the grocery store?" I'm astonished by how upset she appears.

"Lexi?" Her strides appear to be getting longer bringing her to me quicker. "Do you know who goes to the grocery store?"

I roll my eyes at her. Of course, I know. I go to the grocery store. The closer she gets, the stronger my will to escape becomes. I try the door handle again, only to discover the inevitable. It's still locked. Banging my fist against the door, I turn back to Haley and face her wrath.

"What's the problem?" She makes it to my side quickly dismissing the grocery store and overlooking how pissed she seemed only seconds ago.

"It's locked." I glance back at the door, defeat riddled in my tone. "It's weird because it's the only one that is." I wave my hand at the rest of the doors.

"Let me see." Haley reaches for the handle as if her touch can magically spring the lock. Perhaps she does possess that ability. To be honest, it wouldn't surprise me if she did. Haley jiggles the handle and pushes against the door. Nothing happens. She bends down to examine the lock.

I follow her lead, bending at the waist to inspect the simple mechanism preventing me from entering the room. Disbelief courses through me when I see the type of lock barring me. Straightening, I quickly turn and march down the hallway at a swift pace.

"Where are you going?" Haley calls as she messes with the door.

"I'll be right back. Stay here."

I thump down the stairs taking them two at a time but take extra precaution when rounding the corner leading to the living room. Passing through that room, I trek down the hallway and back into Landon's office. Striding straight over to the desk, I pull the chair back, pull the last drawer on the right open, reach in and pull out the wooden box. Placing the box on the desk I open the lid and reach for the black velvet sack. Ripping open the drawstring I reach in, grab the skeleton key, and drop the sack back into the box before I take off running back upstairs.

Haley is leaning against the wall waiting.

I run up to her, waving the key in my excitement. Reaching the door, I insert the key in the lock and turn it. Presto, the key works. As I turn the handle to open the door, Haley grabs my arm.

"Do you think this is his playroom?" she asks.

Honestly, it didn't occur to me he would have a playroom here but, I suppose if he has a bedroom for his subs it would only stand to reason he would have a playroom too. I hesitate to open the door.

Do I want to know if it is his playroom?

Do I want to see it?

Hell, yes. I nudge the door, letting it swing open and I'm confronted with yet another shocking revelation. It's definitely not a playroom. Glancing around, the room resembles a broadcast center, the kind you see on television shows where the audience is behind the scenes. The room is smaller than his office. Along the back wall is a long table serving as a desk, with two computer chairs positioned side-by-side in front of it. On the wall above the table are dozens of monitors that start at the top of the desk and climb as high as the ceiling. They are stacked four screens high and six screens wide.

I move into the room to investigate further. As I approach the long table I see two keyboards along with their mouse partners sitting in front of each chair.

Haley steps in and examines the room.

"What the hell is this?" she asks, pulling the question straight out of my head.

"My thoughts exactly." I walk over to the table and survey all of the equipment.

Unexpectedly, things start to come alive. Hard drives whiz to life. Monitors flash and display images. I glance at Haley who is watching the scene in front of us as closely as I am.

When the first screen is visible and the scene becomes clearer I step in for a closer look not believing my eyes. In the tiny screen I can make out Landon's night club. This particular camera is situated inside the room where Leroy greets us.

Shocked, I turn and look at Haley to gauge her reaction.

Her eyes narrow the longer she stares at the screen.

I view the next monitor as it comes into focus. The elevator in the club. I almost feel relief because it confirms my hunch—we were being watched. Seeing it firsthand is downright disturbing. I quickly monitor all the displays. A majority of them give me an unobstructed view of

Landon's club. Two are surveillance of this house, one of the front gate, and the other of the front door. Resuming my sweep, I target the last couple of ones and gasp in shock, taking a step back.

"What is it?" Haley reaches out to steady my shaking form. I almost fall over backwards as I take small steps.

"Look, Haley." I point to the incriminating images.

There, at the bottom left hand corner, on one of the screens, is my living room on display for everyone to see. Okay, maybe not everyone, but it sure feels like everyone. And, above that screen is another—this one is exhibiting my bedroom. My bedroom, for crying out loud. The one on top of that is my front door. Stunned. I am too stunned to speak. My knees grow week. I think I might pass out.

"Here, sit down." Haley pulls out a chair motioning me to sit.

Plopping down into the chair, my eyes are glued to the displays if for no other reason than to verify what I'm seeing is real. And sure enough, it's my house presenting itself back at me. *What the hell?*

"What is this, Haley?"

"I don't know." Her voice sounds anguished so I glance at her.

She frantically searches all the screens. For what, I have no idea.

"Where's this?" She points to a screen.

I look at the display her finger is aimed at, trying to figure out what or where the place is, to no avail. I have no idea where it is as I lean closer to the screen noticing it looks like a club of some sort. Although, the element at this club is certainly not like Landon's club.

This club appears run down, shabby, and obviously serves a lower class of customers or members—whatever they are classified as in this establishment. It's mid-afternoon so clients are minimal but there are a few people hanging around what is probably the front entrance. There is a girl sitting off to one side at a pass-through portion of the wall collecting coats, I assume by the rack of coats stationed directly behind her. A few clients/customers have just arrived and bypass the girl on their way into the club.

"What club do you think that is?" I ask Haley hoping she can shed some light on this discovery.

"I have no idea," Haley replies with such disdain in her voice.

It is foolish of me to think she would have any knowledge of a place so beneath her social status but you never know. She has surprised me in the past. Just recently in fact.

Haley takes the chair beside me and leans closer to the monitors.

I browse all the other gadgets spread across the table. There are three panels with a ton of buttons and a lot of sliding knobs on each of them. I lean over for a better view and press the button closest to me.

"What happened?" Haley glimpses at me then at the screens again.

I evaluate the screens and notice all of the displays have changed to different locations in the club and my house. I press the button again and they return to their original shots.

"How many cameras do you think he has?" I think out loud as I move onto the next button and press it.

"Do you think you should be touching those?" Haley examines the buttons as I glance her way. "I'm just saying we don't know anything about this system. It could trigger alarms or something." I glare at her. "What? You never know." She waves her hand at the monitors.

She's right.

Damn it.

I remove my fingers from the buttons and go back to looking at the screens. Still in quite a bit of shock, I examine the three showcasing my house. Front door, living room and bedroom are all visible as I try to figure out where the cameras are placed. To know that he has been watching me is freaking me out. I want to know why? *Why would he put cameras in my house? How did he do this?*

Haley and I sit silently, mesmerized by the monitors in front of us.

A voice from the hallway startles us both, and I jump a little in my seat.

"Hello," Mrs. Howard calls out from down the hall.

I jump out of my chair and run to the door, then go out into the hall to see Mrs. Howard making her way toward me.

"Oh, there you are. Are you and your friend almost done?" She seems a bit agitated.

"Yes, Mrs. Howard. We won't be long," I say hoping to calm her uneasiness a little.

"Oh, that's good, dear. Would you like to stay for a late lunch?"

"Sure, we'd like that," I answer for both of us which will probably send Haley over the edge, but she'll get over it.

"Good, it'll be ready in twenty minutes. I hope you'll be done with whatever you are doing by then?" Her eyes dash to the room behind me.

"Absolutely, we'll be down soon."

Mrs. Howard peeks around the door to the room we are occupying. Her gaze meets mine for a moment before she turns around and waddles back to the staircase. I stand watching her make her way down the stairs making certain she is gone before I return to the room.

Haley remains fixed in the same seat viewing the screens diligently.

I make my way back to reclaim the chair I previously occupied and examine all the displays once more.

Music breaks the silence in the room.

I turn to Haley who shrugs her shoulders, stands up, pulls her phone out of her back pocket and slides her finger across the front of the screen.

I return my attention to the monitors, this time concentrating on Landon's club. I figure there has to be something in there that can help us—there has to be. Since it is early afternoon there aren't many clients around, but Landon's employees are manning the place. It's still unbelievable to me that it's business as usual there. It seems wrong.

"I got it. Yes." Haley's aggravated voice demands my attention as I glance at her. She is pacing the room, listening to whoever is on the phone. "Look, I asked you to look into it. Nothing more." Her voice raises in volume. I watch as she continues to pace the room. "Fine. Yes I understand." She slides her finger across the screen and holds her phone up to her forehead as she stands still with her eyes closed.

"Haley? What is it?" I call out hoping to snap her out of her trance.

"What?" She acknowledges me.

I stare at her waiting for some sort of explanation. When it's apparent none is forthcoming, I press further.

"Who was that?" I'm troubled by her strange behavior.

"Nobody." She walks over to resume sitting in the chair beside me.

I glare at her wondering what she's hiding from me.

Haley intensely studies the monitors. "Do you know what that place is?" She focuses back on the screen as if the phone call never happened.

"Yeah, that's Landon's garage."

"Garage?" She turns to look at me.

"Yeah, Landon has a couple of cars in there."

"Hmmm."

"What?" I don't understand her fixation on the garage.

"Nothing. Just thinking." Haley returns to examining the screens. "Hit that button again."

"What button?"

"The button that switches the view of the cameras."

I reach over and hit the button switching the views.

Haley scans over each display quickly. "Shit." She jumps

up knocking her chair backwards. "Come on, we have to go."

"What are you talking about?" I'm completely shocked by her actions. "Haley, what's going on?"

"Jesus Christ, Lexi. Listen to me. We have to go." She turns and starts for the door.

"No."

She halts her steps and turns around.

"Tell me what is going on? What did you see? Who did you talk to?"

"Fine." Haley marches back, stops beside me and points at one of the screens. "Do you recognize that place?"

I lean closer to the one she is pointing at for a closer inspection. "Holy shit." Now it's my turn to jump out of my chair as I back away from what's in front of me. "How can that be?"

Staring at the screen, the scene in front of me is so familiar it's scary. I'm staring at the restaurant where Haley and I frequently have lunch. The view is of the entire parking lot, and the front door. I stare in astonishment, speechless, wondering what the hell is going on here?

"Is he a stalker?" I say out loud, to no one in particular.

"I don't think so," Haley whispers as she glances around the room.

"What are you doing?"

"Looking for cameras." She moves to the corner of the room inspecting the ceiling. She comes back over to stand next to me, but is still viewing the room.

"Lexi. Whatever is going on here? Whatever Landon

and these men are involved in? It's dangerous. These people are running an exclusive club. This club is a cover for whatever is going on." Haley waves her arm across the displays.

She's upset, scared. I've never seen her this way before.

"I realize that, Haley."

"No. I don't think you do." She leans down coming face-to-face with me. "Whatever these men are doing is most likely illegal. We can't continue with this. We need to go now."

Haley storms over to the door once again.

I sit back down and resume staring at the monitors.

"Lexi? Let's go. Now." Haley stands at the door waiting for me to follow, but I can't.

"Lexi?" She calls out again, anger rising in her tone.

"Haley. I can't."

"You can." She swiftly crosses the room to stand in front of me again. "And, you will. I got you involved in this and I'm going to get you out. Now, let's go." She grabs my arm trying to drag me from the room.

"Haley, stop." I remain seated, refusing to move.

"Don't you get it? Don't you see what's going on here?" Her arm is frantically waving at the screens again. "Landon's involved with that man. And that phone call I just got was from a friend filling me in on Alistair and his associates." Haley sits back down and leans towards me as she talks in a lower voice. "This Alistair guy is into everything, Lexi. Drugs. Women. Killing. He's the damn Mob. And not just in the Mob, Lexi. He's their leader, straight from Italy. We have to go. Now." Haley gets up again, and walks quickly to the door.

I remain still.

Haley stops once she's in the hallway and turns to see if I'm following. "I'm leaving. Are you coming?"

I can't believe it's come to this. I can't believe we're here, fighting about something so—I don't even have words. I peek up at Haley, meeting her eyes. And, she knows by the look on my face and by my body language, I'm not going to follow her this time. She knows I can't follow her.

"It's your funeral."

Those are her final words before she disappears out of sight.

CHAPTER 21

*T*he rustling coming from the scanner brings my attention back to the here and now. The sounds of Landon going about his morning seep through the speaker. There's water running which I assume is him showering.

I glance around this room seeking out Dalton, whom it seems has disappeared. I listen to the sounds in this house for a moment before hearing the cascade of running water coming from down the hall and realize Dalton is in the bathroom, showering.

My attention returns to the scanner as I listen for any signs of life besides water running, but there are none.

Footsteps coming down the hallway, alert me to Dalton's return.

"Did I miss anything?" He probes teasingly.

"Nope."

He stops behind me, messes with my hair as he leans

over to pick up his car keys. "I won't be long." He walks to the front door.

"The closest store is an hour away."

"True. But I drive fast." He flashes a devious smile at me from the door to the hallway. "Besides, you'll be too busy watching that black box to notice I'm gone." He laughs as he points at the scanner.

"That's not true."

He gives me a pointed look.

"Fine. It's a little true," I laugh, slightly. "But, I still don't see why I can't come with you."

"You know why." All signs of humor disappears.

"Yeah, right. No one can see me. Blah, blah, blah." I repeat the speech as I get up and move to the window. "You're like a broken record."

Dalton laughs as he walks down the hall and out the front door.

I remain at the window staring out, while listening to the rustling noises coming from the scanner. Landon is moving around doing only Lord knows what. I glance at the clock and realize it's later than I expected it to be then peer down at myself and see my pajamas.

I rush down the hall to my room ripping my sleepwear off and throwing on jeans and a T-shirt. I go into the bathroom, whip my hair into a ponytail and start brushing my teeth mortified that I hadn't done this before leaning into Dalton and blasting him with my morning breath. As I'm scrubbing my teeth thoroughly, I hear a commotion coming from the scanner and stop mid-brush to listen.

I hear a door bang and footsteps on what sounds like a concrete or tiled floor.

"You ready?" An unknown voice pours out of the scanner.

"Yes." Landon's tone is clipped, agitated.

That one small word immediately reminds me why we're here. It washes away any self-pity I've had about being stuck in this house.

I hear two sets of footsteps marching along, a door shutting and more shoes pounding the floor.

I hear what sounds like a scuffle.

I rinse quickly, wipe a towel across my mouth before dropping it on the vanity and running to the kitchen table. The sounds become louder and more aggressive. An awful thudding noise fills the room, as I hurry to look out the window.

Landon is on the ground, curled up into a ball, while holding his side.

The guard is circling him.

I'm terrified, thinking they've found his listening device while I watch helplessly.

"You really are stupid. Aren't you?" The guard growls as he lifts his leg, giving Landon a kick to his stomach.

Landon lets out a small whimper and is jolted by the kick.

The guard bends down and yanks Landon by the hair, hoisting his head up so they are face-to-face.

"I should kill you right now."

That's it for me. That's all I can take as I run to my room, slip on my running shoes, and grab my pepper spray off the dresser on the way out the door. I make my way to Dalton's room, coming to a halt in front of the night stand next to his bed, I open the drawer and pull out his gun. Shoving the gun down the back of my pants I take off out the front door running toward the wall of stone.

I don't think. I don't consider how I will get into this fortress. I just run across the lawn, until I'm at the stone wall. I jump up barely reaching the top, but manage to grab a hold of it and haul myself over in one swoop, impressing even myself. I have no time to pat myself on the back as I run toward Landon and the guard.

As I get close enough, I slow to a jog and look ahead to see what is happening.

Landon is still on the ground and the guard standing above him.

I pick up the pace until I'm about five feet from them. I stop, pull the gun out of my pants and aim it for the guard's head.

The guard is preparing to kick Landon again.

"Stop right there," I yell out.

The guard halts his movements and spins around.

"Don't. Move."

The guard peers at me, eyes narrowed.

"Put your hands up where I can see them."

The guard appraises me for a moment before he laughs. A huge belly laugh which only aggravates me further.

"Do as I say or I will shoot."

In a heavy Italian accent the guard speaks to me. "Lady, you have no idea what kind of trouble you're bringing on yourself." He laughs even harder.

"Thanks you for your concern, but I know exactly what I'm doing." I cock the gun. "Face in the dirt."

The guard looks astonished as he drops to his knees, peering around the property, looking for his backup no doubt.

What he doesn't realize is that it's time for the guards to switch shifts—but I do. There is a five minute window when the guards are coming and going. If I'm going to get Landon out of here—now is the time.

The guard lies face down on the ground.

"Hands behind your head," I order.

He places them behind his head, cussing the entire time.

I finally let my gaze wander to Landon who is lying on his side, holding his stomach and staring up at me. For a minute I think he's angry, in fact, I know he's angry, but I don't care. Dalton will be angry too, but again, I don't care.

I move over to Landon and kneel down at his side while watching the guard.

"Can you stand?"

Landon coughs a few times before he's able to talk. "Yeah. I think so."

I grab his arm, ready to help him to his feet.

"We have to hurry, Landon." I glance around the property. Everything is clear so far. "Come on, get up."

I pull his arm and he struggles to stand. Once on his feet, he stares at me in awe before reaching out and running his hand over my cheek.

"What are you doing here?" he asks.

"Not now. We don't have time for this. We have to go." I attempt to pull him along but he doesn't budge. "Landon?"

"Lexi, I can't leave." His voice is soft, apologetic.

"Yes, Landon. You can. And, you will. Now let's go," I tug on his arm once again.

"Lexi, you don't understand," he argues as he remains immobile.

"Can we discuss this later? We have to go. Now."

Landon begins cussing under his breath, then begins talking to whom I assume is Lawrence.

"Yes. She's here now." He listens for a moment. "How the hell did this happen?"

"Landon?" I call out to get his attention.

He glances at me.

"We have to move," I urge him.

At last, he begins to walk in the direction I'm dragging him. I take one last look at the guard, making certain he remains on the ground as we begin moving.

"Do you think you can run?" I ask Landon as I pick up the pace.

"We'd better. We only have two minutes before this place is surrounded by guards again." My head snaps to his. "Don't ask."

We both start running for the wall.

Coming upon it, I freeze and glance at Landon. I know he's hurt and this will be difficult for him.

"Can you make it?"

"Yes. Ladies first." He waves the hand not holding his side toward the wall.

I'm not stupid and I'm not going first.

"No. Let's be sure you can make it." I indicate for him to go first.

"Touché, Mrs. Shaw." He steps up.

"It's Ms. Waters, now."

Landon jumps up, grabs the top of the wall and pulls himself over.

I step forward, ready to jump when I feel cold metal against the back of my head.

"Your turn." I hear Landon call out.

A body presses against mine and I feel breath behind my ear.

"Don't say a word." The heavy thick accent breaths into my ear. A hand reaches around my body, grabbing hold of my gun and pulls it from my hand.

I remain perfectly still.

"You coming, Ms. Waters?" Landon calls out. When I don't answer he tries again. "Lexi?"

The breath in my ear exhales. "Shhh."

I remain silent and still as I hear Landon jump up to grab the top of the wall.

The guard leans forward and peeks up at the top of the wall.

I pick up my foot, then stomp it heavily onto his. As he hobbles, in obvious pain, I elbow him in the stomach which causes him to drop on the ground. Spinning around, I pull the pepper spray out of my front pocket, raise it to his eyes and spray.

The guard cries out in agony as Landon drops down from the wall. He comes to me immediately, cupping my face in his hands.

"Are you okay?" He strokes my face.

"Yes. I'm fine." I move us toward the wall. "Come on. Let's go," I state. "Together."

Landon nods at me.

I step forward at the same time as he does. We both jump and grab the top, hauling ourselves over. Landing on the other side, we both stand together, then turn to make our getaway.

We come face to face with the barrels of shot guns.

We both put our hands up slowly.

"Throw over the pepper spray, little lady," another heavy-accented guard says. I reach behind me to pull it out of my pocket.

"Slowly."

I pull the container out, bring it around the front of me and toss it to them. There are three guards holding guns to our heads.

"Jesus Christ," Landon mumbles under his breath.

I peek over at him to see his eyes narrowed to slits and his brows knitted together.

"Move," one of the guards orders, bringing my attention back to all three gun-wielding guards.

One of them motions to our right, so I move slowly in that direction.

"Hands behind your heads," the guard snaps at us.

We all start heading in the direction of the front gates.

Landon is angry.

The guards have itchy trigger fingers.

My mind is running circles thinking of how I am going to get us out of here.

*a*s we reach the front gates of the compound, a guard steps out of small stone booth, while speaking Italian to the others.

I glance at Landon to see him whispering, but can't make out what he is saying.

The guard who emerges from the booth speaks to Landon, but once again, he speaks in Italian, and I'm at a loss for his foreign words.

Landon tugs my arm, dragging me to the stone wall. "On your knees," he commands as he drops to his, pressing his body against the wall, turns his face and scowls at me.

I follow suit and drop to my knees, placing my cheek against the wall so I'm facing Landon. I hear the guards talking amongst themselves and want desperately to look over at them but refrain.

"What are you doing here?" Landon growls.

He's angry.

"I came to help you," I whisper.

"And, what makes you think I need help?"

His voice is cold and sterile—just as unfeeling as that night he hurt me. I don't know how to answer him, so I don't. My eyes remain fixed on his trying to make him understand. Understand I'm here to help him. Understand how I couldn't stay away. Understand the fact that I love him.

Sadly, it appears he doesn't. His eyes remain cold and fixed on mine.

I close my eyes so I will no longer see the pure anger burning in his.

"What do we have here?" the voice I prayed I'd never hear again fills my ears. "So, the two lovebirds are together again." Alistair's voice is chilling.

Landon squeezes his eyes.

"Jesus Christ. Jesus Christ. Jesus Christ," he mumbles.

"What was that Landon?" Alistair asks a little too cheery for my liking.

Landon remains silent, eyes still closed.

"Answer me," Alistair commands.

"Jesus Christ, Sir," Landon says through clenched teeth.

I watch, helplessly as Alistair takes three strides forward to stand behind Landon.

"Look at me." The anger in his voice is evident.

My eyes dart to Landon, as I nervously await his response.

Slowly he opens his eyes, turns his head and glares at Alistair.

"What did you call me?" Alistair barks.

"I'm sorry. Master," Landon spits out the title like venom.

"I see more training in your future, my beautiful boy." Alistair pets Landon's hair like a dog.

The words 'beautiful boy' register in my mind. Those words are familiar, like I should know them. And, then it dawns on me. That's what Jason called Landon on the night he attacked me at the club. I revert my attention back to these two.

"How many infractions are we looking at here?" Alistair turns and begins pacing behind Landon and me. "Trying to escape." He begins ticking his fingers as he talks. "Calling me the wrong name. Making my men here work harder than they should have to. Upsetting my entire day. Holding a gun on my men."

I interject at this point.

"That was me," I blurt out then mentally slap myself.

Alistair, who is on the other side of Landon with his back to me, whips around to face me. Taking the two steps to bring himself to my side, he halts his movement. "What did you say?" he asks, bewildered by my intrusion.

"I said I was the one with the gun." My voice remains calm, not betraying how absolutely terrified I am.

Alistair rubs his chin with his fingers like he's thinking. Abruptly, he turns back to Landon. "She's pretty brave. I can see why you keep her around."

Landon growls as he glares at Alistair.

Alistair looks back to me. "What to do with you?" he asks, as if it's a question. I'm not buying it. Whatever he plans to do with me he already knows, there's no decision to be made. This is all for show.

My eyes meet Alistair's.

"Foolish little girl." He clicks his tongue in disgust. "I would've thought you learned your lesson the last time we met."

"Not even close," I spit out.

Alistair laughs. "Feisty one, aren't you." He reaches out, pulls my head back by my hair and slaps me across the face. Hard.

Pain spreads across my cheek as I stumble. I hold my face as tears spring to my eyes. I refuse to let them spill over as I take a deep breath and bringing myself back to my knees. I jut out my chin and shoot Alistair a menacing look.

He looks impressed—almost giddy by my defiance.

I leverage a threatening look to match his scorn.

Landon struggles to remain still.

"Don't move," Alistair commands Landon, pointing a finger at him. "She'll pay dearly if you do."

Alistair turns to his men. "Go now." A nod of his head points them toward the house I've been staying in.

I close my eyes, praying I'm wrong and he doesn't know.

Alistair shifts back to us. "What shall we do while we wait?" He smirks.

"What are we waiting for?" I ask.

Alistair sneers at me, then faces Landon. "You'll never train this one." He points at me. "I'll be doing you a favor when I kill her."

Landon growls again.

"Down boy," Alistair warns again.

Landon reins in his anger. This earns him another petting.

I close my eyes, refusing to watch this display.

"I should just kill you too." Alistair intimidates with a deadly whisper. "You've been more trouble than you're worth," he muses. Gliding his hand along one side of Landon's face, he cups his chin and twists Landon's head toward him.

To watch Alistair touch Landon so intimately, like a lover, makes my skin crawl. I wonder for the millionth time what the true story is. *What is really going on here? Why would Landon come here—voluntarily?*

"But…" He lets go of Landon's chin and begins pacing again. "You're my biggest challenge and I will break you," he vows, facing Landon and regarding him with a scowl.

I see the struggle within Landon not to say or do anything. Unfortunately, I don't possess that much control.

"You're an animal," I yell out. "He's not a dog."

"Jesus, woman. Don't you know when to close your mouth?" Alistair snarls at me.

"Don't." Landon growls—at me.

He growled at me?

What the hell?

"It's too bad you won't have that challenge, Landon." Alistair points at me again. " There's no greater feeling in the world than seeing someone break before your very eyes. She'd be quite the challenge for you." He smiles at Landon. "Perhaps, I'll let you keep her as a pet." He rubs his chin again, like he's actually considering it. "You'd have to train her though. She can't be this way." He waves his hand at me with a sinister smile.

I'm stunned. Is this evil man really considering making me a pet for his pet? Seriously? What the hell kind of place is this?

My head snaps around to the sound of gravel crunching under tires. Looking in the direction of the driveway, I see a black SUV coming up the driveway at an accelerated speed. All the windows are tinted black making it impossible to see who is inside. I see something come out of the sunroof landing on the ground three feet away from us.

Suddenly, there is a flash of light as I feel someone slam into me knocking me to the ground. Smoke fills the air around us as another flash goes off and even more smoke engulfs us. Through the dense fog, I barely detect a head of blond hair and a pair of arms waving frantically. Landon grabs me, pulling me to my feet and we take off running towards the vehicle.

My eyes are stinging, a stream of tears pour out of them. But, when I pry them open, I see my salvation in the form of Dalton who is sporting two machine guns which he holds at his sides and fires randomly.

We make it to him as he steps back towards the SUV.

"Get in," he yells out.

Landon and I make our way around the vehicle as shots ring out everywhere. I yank the passenger door open, and scramble in, ducking down. I peek between the seats to the backseat to make sure Landon made it too. I sigh in relief seeing Landon in the backseat, but immediately panic as I look out the driver's side window for Dalton.

When I don't see him standing there, I crawl over to the driver's side and glance out the window all around the area of the car. At the back door, Dalton is near the back door, against the vehicle, firing his weapons.

"Landon?" I shout out as I quickly sit in the seat and fasten my seatbelt. "Open the door for Dalton."

Landon slides across the seat, whipping open the door and sliding out of the way. Dalton dives in the car, drops his guns on the floor, while I slam the SUV into reverse and step on the gas.

Speeding backwards down the driveway I hit the road and spin the car around, slamming the gearshift into drive before pressing the gas pedal to the floor. Shots are ringing out all around us as I speed down the road.

All is quiet in the car but I can feel a storm brewing.

I speed down the road pushing the pedal to the metal so to speak. Checking the rear-view mirror every few seconds, to see whether cars are following us, there are none as of yet. I glance at the speedometer to find the needle buried. I ease my foot off the gas and look out the rear-view mirror once more. Just to double-check, I take a glimpse out the side view mirror. No cars are following us. I slow the car a wee bit more to a respectable 150 mph.

"Turn left up here," Landon calls out from the back seat.

"No stay on this road," Dalton contradicts.

"Which way?" I ask confused.

"Lexi. Make a left." Landon leans forward in the seat,

and I can feels his eyes on me. "Trust me," he says as the road in question comes up.

"Who got you this far?" Dalton brags.

I don't know what to do as the road is coming up fast and my mind is tossing around who to trust. Who to believe. I slow the car as we come upon the road in question. Not listening to either of them, I make a right.

"Where are you going?" Dalton calls out.

"What the hell are you doing?" Landon shouts. "She's going right. She took a right. Damn it," he's yelling louder now and not speaking to me.

I follow the roadway still peeking in the rear-view mirror and glancing at the side mirror. Still, no other vehicles in sight.

"You two better get on the same page and fast because I'm not listening to either of you if you're going to fight about everything," I say, as a matter of fact.

Stepping on the gas, I keep the car at 100 mph now that I'm sure we aren't being followed.

Up ahead I see something in the roadway, or should I say across the roadway.

"What is that?" I point straight ahead.

"Location?" I hear Landon ask.

"What are you talking about?" I question.

"He's not talking to you." Dalton leans between the seats to look out the windshield. "Slow down, Lexi," he says as he peers ahead.

"No, don't," Landon instructs.

I'm getting aggravated. These two aren't helping they're actually hindering our situation.

"What is that?"

"Looks like a roadblock?" Dalton offers.

"Should I stop?" I glance in the rear-view mirror, only now, spotting the cars coming up behind us—fast.

"Shit—" I blurt out.

"What?" Dalton turns in his seat to glance out the back window. "Shit." He repeats. "Where are your men, Landon?"

I glance at Landon in the backseat.

"That's them ahead of us," he says, then says under his breath. "I think."

We're screwed.

We have cars coming up behind us fast.

Cars blocking the road in front of us.

I don't know what to do.

"Are you sure they're your people, Landon?" I ask.

"Location?" Landon yells out.

"Oh forget it." I yank the steering wheel to the right —hard.

"What the hell are you doing?" Landon yells, as I veer the car to the right into the open field beside us.

We bump along the field.

"What's the plan, Lexi?" Dalton asks a little calmer than Landon.

I glance in the rear-view mirror to see the cars behind us following and the cars in the roadblock have joined too.

We're so screwed.

I see no way out of this.

Landon and Dalton are hanging on for dear life. Each of them has one hand on the seat and the other on the roof of the car as we bounce along the field.

"Stop the car," Landon demands.

"What?" Both Dalton and I reply simultaneously.

"Stop the car," Landon repeats. "Those are my people on the right back there."

"So?" Dalton growls.

"So. We have a plan. Stop the car, Alexandria."

I peer at Landon through the rear-view mirror and see the determination in his eyes.

I glance at Dalton whose eyes are pleading with me to keep going.

I slow the car down as I watch Dalton close his eyes, disappointment and defeat crossing his features.

I pull the car to a halt, throwing the gearshift into park. I take a deep breath before turning around to face the two men in the backseat.

"What now?" I want to know Landon's plan.

"Now. I get out of the car and you two take off," he commands us, then goes back to talking to his people. "Yeah. I'm coming out in a minute. You guys ready?"

I peer at Dalton, silently asking him to do something.

He rolls his eyes at me, shaking his head in disappointment.

"I'm not letting you get out of this car alone," I vow.

"You will do as you are told," he growls at me. "Is that not how we ended up here in the first place?" He gives me a pointed glare. "You not doing what you were told?"

"Don't talk to her like that," Dalton retaliates.

"Don't even get me started on you." Landon regards Dalton with such animosity, it's scary.

"When I exit this car, you step on the gas and get out of

here. Do you hear me, Alexandria?" The penetrating stare he gives me feels like daggers to my heart.

I simply stare back.

"Do I make myself clear?" he shouts causing both Dalton and me to jump.

"Fine," I concede defeated.

"All right. I'm ready," Landon states to whomever is listening in his ear piece. "I'm stepping out now."

He jerks the door handle, swings the door open and steps out. He raises his hands in surrender. My gaze snaps to Dalton who is watching Landon, then out the back window where I see Landon's men at the rear right-hand side of the car. Alistair and his men are at the rear left-hand side of our vehicle.

I feel torn, lost, not a clue what to do in this situation. My father taught me a lot of things; how to fight an attacker, how to shoot a gun, even how to get out of the trunk of a car. Yet, in all our training, in all the times he told me what to do in different situations, never once was being chased by the Mob while being shot at, one of those situations.

The back door to the SUV slams shut, jolting me back to the moment at hand. I look back at Dalton who is still staring at the vehicle door.

"Dalton?"

He turns his head to look at me.

"Should I drive away?"

"Wait a minute." He spins around on the seat to watch out the back window.

Both sides are now out of their vehicles pointing guns

at each other. I've never seen anything like this in my entire life. My heart is pounding in my chest, but I ignore it and search for Landon. He's standing behind our vehicle.

"We have to help him."

"I don't think he wants our help," Dalton retorts.

"I don't care. You can take off. Get out of here if you want. I won't blame you," I reassure him.

"I'm not leaving you here." He sounds shocked by my suggestion as he waves his hand at the back window. "With them."

The standoff outside continues and inside this vehicle.

*a*s Dalton and I debate what to do, the standoff outside intensifies. I glance out the rear-view mirror and see Landon standing at the back of our SUV, his body language revealing everything. He is tense. In attack mode. His back muscles ripple every time he moves. I roll down the window in order to hear what is going on.

Landon's men are on the right side out the back of our truck, led by Leroy. They are standing their ground against Alistair's men who are on the left side, all watching Leroy's team, with the exception of Alistair. He's talking to Landon.

"All of this is unnecessary, Landon," Alistair calls out.

"It won't be if you let them all go," Landon replies.

Alistair laughs manically before he stops all together and narrows his eyes at Landon.

"That's not possible." He waves his hands around the area. "They know too much to allow them to simply walk out of here."

"They know nothing," Landon counters.

Alistair takes two big strides toward Landon.

I hear Leroy's voice call out. "I wouldn't do that if I were you."

I peek back through the rear windshield at Leroy.

He stands at the ready, a gun aimed straight at Alistair's head.

This whole situation is quickly getting out of control.

I fling the driver's side door open, jump out and make my way to the back of the SUV to stand next to Landon.

It's like a scene out of the *Godfather* movies. Both sides are armed—ready to shoot at the slightest command. I should be scared. I should be driving this car away from here as fast as I can, but I feel responsible for the entire situation. If not for me, none of us would be here.

"Get back in the car and do as I asked you to," Landon barks, without so much as a glance in my direction. His eyes are locked on Alistair.

"No," I defy him.

"Alexandria, do as I ask. Please." His eyes remain on Alistair.

"I'm not leaving without you." I survey the scene in front of us.

Alistair is five feet away from us. The rest of the men are fifteen feet or more back. They are all watching each other, only Alistair has his eyes on us. I glare at him as his eyes shift to mine.

"And, I am not leaving here without you." Dalton stands in front of me facing Alistair.

"Jesus Christ," Landon mumbles.

"Looks like you have a small problem, Landon." Alistair takes another step closer to us. "I could take care of these nuisances for you. Just say the word."

"Stay where you are," Landon growls. "I'll handle this."

Landon's eyes remain fixed on Alistair.

"Don't make another move." Dalton raises his gun and points it straight at Alistair's head.

"Such chivalry, wouldn't you say? Helping the damsel in distress." Alistair gives Dalton a sinister smile.

"Just keeping the world safe from the likes of you." Dalton takes aim.

"Watch your tone, boy. You won't like me when I'm angry." Alistair takes another step forward.

"One more move and I'll blow your head off," Dalton warns.

"Is that so?" Alistair is about take another step, but stops when the sound of another vehicle approaching interrupts.

All eyes turn to the vehicle in question as it comes flying across the field kicking up dirt and creating a mini sandstorm. The flying earth is so thick it's difficult to see the vehicle creating it.

The car finally comes to a halt and all eyes are glued to it.

Promptly, the door springs open and a man steps out.

Dalton visibly stiffens in front of me as he watches the man emerge from the vehicle. I peek around his arm for a better view, but don't recognize the man at all. Dalton does and holds his gun trained on Alistair as he addresses the newcomer.

"What are you doing here?" Dalton asks.

Landon peeks over at Dalton with a disgusted look on his face.

I'm completely in the dark not knowing who this new arrival is or what everyone is even more on edge about.

"Did you two really think you could come to my country without me knowing?" Alistair snarls at Dalton. "Did you think you could sit not one mile from my home and watch me without my knowledge?"

Dalton completely ignores Alistair all of his attention on the newcomer.

"You haven't answered my question?" he calls out.

"I told you fifteen years ago to let this go. I told you to stay away from this case. You should've listened to me," the newcomer answers Dalton as he strides forward stopping next to Alistair.

"Some FBI agent you were," Landon growls. "You don't even have a clue what is going." He turns to Dalton. "Do you?"

Dalton shifts his weight, but his glare remains on the other man.

"He's Alistair's brother." Landon waves his hand at the new arrival, disgust heavy in his tone.

Dalton turns to Landon.

"What?"

"He." Landon points at the man. "Is Alistair's brother." The look Landon gives Dalton is pure hatred.

"He can't be." Dalton turns his attention back to the man —Alistair's brother apparently. "You were the head of our office at the FBI," Dalton says.

I'm shocked—stunned actually, as I peer over at

Dalton's boss, ex-boss, or whatever he is. That part of Dalton's story, the part when he brought Landon back to the States begins to fall into place. How he didn't know what happened when he landed in the US? Why he was taken off Landon's case so abruptly? It all makes sense now with the arrival of Alistair's brother.

I step beside Dalton to look at his face, see his reaction but his expression is unmoving as stone, displaying nothing. I can't imagine what is running through his mind. To find out your boss, the head of the FBI New York office, is not who he's been portrayed to be is hard enough. But, to realize you've been made a fool out of too, must be devastating.

Dalton stands, gun aimed at Alistair, but his fierce look directed at his brother.

Landon scoffs as he steps toward Dalton. "He can be and he is," he declares. "Now, take Alexandria. Get in the car and drive away from here," Landon demands through clenched teeth.

"I'm not going without you." I don't know why he doesn't understand this.

Landon runs his hand through his hair as he sighs.

"No one is going anywhere." Alistair's bother speaks for the first time.

"There's no win here." Landon turns to the brothers. "If you don't let them go my men will have no other choice but to start firing."

I glance at all the men behind the brothers. Leading the pack on Landon's side is Leroy with his gun still aimed at

Alistair. Alistair's men are just as prepared as I see their leader with his gun trained on Landon.

My heart pounding in my chest is loud in my ears and I wonder how this will end. There's no way I can see. It's not as if these people are going to let us walk out of here. There's not good outcome I can foresee. If we have to shoot our way out, people will die. There's no denying that.

CHAPTER 24

*a*s I look around the area, we are in the middle of a field—a farmer's field by my estimation. There is nothing as far as the eye can see. No houses. Nothing. Escaping this situation will be difficult, if there's any chance to escape at all. As the pounding in my chest slows down, I feel defeat creeping in.

There are fifteen people here. Leroy has four men with him. Alistair has five—seven if you include him and his brother. Then there's Landon, Dalton and I. Everyone has a gun aimed at someone with the exception of Landon, Alistair, his brother and I. That leaves eleven people with guns and these aren't little hand guns you see in the movies. No, some of these are actual machine guns. I had no idea Dalton had that kind of weaponry with him until he brandished them at the castle.

How are we going to get out of this?

That's the thought running through my mind, watching this standoff as if it's happening in slow motion.

Suddenly, Dalton snaps out of whatever stupor he was in.

"How can this be? How did you make it to the top of the FBI?" He growls at Alistair's brother.

"I worked hard. Worked my way up." He shrugs his shoulder

"Plus, it helps to have friends in the right positions," Alistair volunteers.

"What is that supposed to mean?" Dalton addresses Alistair.

"It means there's another brother," Landon says.

"What?" Dalton's eyes never leave the brothers.

"You should've done your homework before you were fired, Dalton." Landon's face is full of disgust. "Know your enemy. That statement should've been drilled into your head being an ex-FBI agent and all," Landon sneers.

What? Dalton's not FBI? How can that be? He was at my house, with other agents. What the hell is going on here?

I look at Dalton who only has eyes for the brothers.

Landon's gaze is fixed on the brothers too.

"You need to get in the car and drive away from here, Lexi," Leroy commands as he looks at Alistair. "Let the woman go, she has no part in this."

Alistair turns to Leroy. "You really think I'm just going to let her out of here?"

"She's done nothing to you. She knows nothing. Let her go," Leroy repeats.

"She knows enough," Alistair says. "You, of all people know what happens to people who know too much. Don't you, Leroy?" Alistair's sinister smile lets me know there is more to what he is saying.

"You better shut up now," Leroy warns, gun aimed at Alistair.

"Why, Leroy? Afraid of what I might say?" Alistair steps closer to Leroy. "What has you in such a state?"

"You move one more muscle consider yourself dead," Leroy threatens.

"Alistair. This is about you and me," Landon speaks, as he takes a step forward, trying to regain control of the situation.

I grab his arm attempting to hold him back, but he shrugs it off.

"I'll come back with you, right now." Landon takes another step forward. "Just let them all go. They have nothing to do with this. They know nothing."

Alistair turns and appraises Landon. They hold each other's gaze for what feels like forever. Out of nowhere Alistair begins laughing. A deep, belly roaring laugh. He actually resembles a madman.

Once his laughter subsides, he takes a step towards Landon.

"Do you think I'm stupid?" He takes another step. "Do you really think you've been fooling me?" Another step. "Do you not know I've been keeping tabs on you all this time?"

He takes another step closer, bringing him within three feet of Landon.

Dalton moves his gun to keep it trained on Alistair, his

eyes darting back and forth between Alistair and his brother.

"I know everything *you* do and everything *you* have done," Landon steps closer to Alistair. "I've been keeping tabs on you too." Landon takes another step. "Everything you've done over the last fifteen years has been recorded, put in a secure location that will be made public if anything happens to me. If you let everyone here go, I'll hand everything over to you. All evidence. All files," Landon offers.

The two stand face to face.

Alistair gazes into Landon's eyes, no doubt attempting to verify his sincerity.

"Now, you see Landon. I want to believe *you*." Alistair steps right in front Landon, runs his fingers along the side of Landon's face. "I really do. We have a special relationship, you and I. Don't we?" Alistair removes his hand from Landon's face.

Landon stiffens.

"But, see. That right there is what makes me not believe a word *you* say." Alistair takes a step back. "When *you* were mine." He scoffs. "Really mine, you didn't flinch. Besides," he leans closer whispering. "Do you not think I know what you've been up to the entire time you've been here?"

Landon stands up taller, squaring his shoulders in an attempt to look imposing. Difficult to achieve considering he is barefoot and only wearing pajama bottoms. Still, I have to say he's standing his ground achieving an air of power and control of the situation.

"Do you think of me as ill-advised, Landon? You really

miscalculated me. I've known all about your earpiece, your microphone, and your friends over there..." Alistair waves his hand at Leroy, "...all along. So don't think you're fooling anybody by coming here voluntarily. I knew you'd never be mine again."

Landon holds Alistair's gaze.

Dalton still holds his gun to Alistair's head while watching his ex-boss.

"Alistair," his brother calls out to him. "Move this along." He turns heading back to his car.

"Stop right there," Dalton calls out as he swings his gun pointing it at Alistair's brother.

Alistair's brother keeps walking.

"I'll shoot, Antonio," Dalton cautions.

Antonio halts, spins around and strides toward Dalton.

"You won't shoot me." His anger is apparent. "I taught you. I commanded you. You don't have it in you."

"Stop now," Dalton warns.

Antonio keeps striding forward.

A shot rings out.

CHAPTER 25

There are times in life when you look back on what you've done and where you've been. Reflecting on everything from what kind of person you are —a life-taker or lifesaver? What kind of morals you have— a cheater, liar, or upstanding citizen? I always thought I was a lifesaver—an upstanding citizen.

But, when I heard that gunshot, I really hoped Dalton had killed the son of bitch. I wanted to watch him die, right in front of my eyes, and I knew I wouldn't lift a finger to help him. Those are my thoughts. So, what kind of person does that make me?

When the shot rang out I covered my ears against the loudness and closed my eyes at the same time. During the few silent moments after the shot, everything is frozen. It's as if time is standing still. There is absolutely no sound. I open my eyes slowly, and much to my disappointment, Antonio is not only alive and well, but he looks even more pissed at Dalton.

The world snaps back into real time and everything around me starts moving again.

And then, all hell breaks loose.

I hear more shots ring out, people shouting, vehicles revving their engines.

Suddenly, arms wrap around my waist, dragging me towards our SUV. I peek up to see Landon shielding me with his body as he flings open the back door nudging me toward safety. I fall in, crouching low on the seat as shots continue to whiz all around us.

The door slams shut, muffling all sound.

A few seconds later the driver's door opens, allowing the sounds of the shooting to ring throughout the car once again. Landon jumps into the driver's seat and slams the door shut just as the back door across from me springs open.

I peek over to see Dalton making his way into the car. I sit up, making room to accommodate him.

He puts one leg in as he begins to sit.

I hear a loud bang in my ears and watch in horror as Dalton is jerked forward into the front passenger seat. He bounces off it and falls into the backseat.

"Dalton?" I scream as I scramble closer, grabbing hold of him. He slumps sideways into my lap. There's blood pouring out of his back by his right shoulder blade. I cover the wound with my hand as I struggle to get his other leg into the vehicle. Bullets are ricocheting off the open back door. "Landon, help me."

Landon throws the SUV into gear and slams on the gas pedal. "Pull him in," he shouts, driving over the bumpy terrain.

"I'm trying to," I yell, as I struggle to keep one hand on Dalton's wound. With my free hand I try to pull his leg further into the SUV—a feat made more difficult by the bouncing of the vehicle.

At last, I get his legs completely in the before I wiggle out from under him, lean over and pull the door shut. Placing my hands back on his wound, I'm thankful he's passed out knowing the pain would be unbearable.

"He's shot, Landon," I yell as I press hard on the wound. "We need a hospital."

"Just keep pressure on the wound," Landon drives at full speed.

Dalton and I are bouncing all around and I struggle to keep us in the seat. He weighs a lot making it harder for me to hold him and stop him from spilling onto the floor.

I glance out the window beside me to see a vehicle attempting to pull up beside us. It's black, with tinted windows preventing us from identifying its occupants.

I glance back at Landon just in time to see him give the steering wheel a hard right. Luckily, I have time to anticipate the shift of the vehicle and hold on tight to Dalton.

We hit a huge bump or pothole, catapulting Dalton and I toward the roof of the SUV. I hit my head before Dalton is wrenched from my arms and thrown to the floor. I land back on the seat hard and bounce a few times. It feels like we're riding a horse as we go bumping along.

Grabbing onto Dalton again, I scoop him back into my arms as the vehicle settles down to a smooth ride.

Glancing out the front windshield I see roadway.

Thank God.

As I gaze out the side window, I no longer see any vehicles trying to approach. I turn a little on the seat and look out the back windshield to discover four or more cars tailing us. One vehicle is attempting to push another off the road. Since all vehicles are black SUV's it's difficult to tell who is who, so I give up and return my attention to Dalton.

He's bleeding profusely evident from all the blood oozing out from under my hands. I search the car spotting a rag tucked in the pouch on the back of the passenger seat. Reaching over, I tug on it releasing it from its snug hold and bring it closer to my face for an inspection. It appears clean with no unusual odors coming from it. I place it over Dalton's wound and press down hard.

"He's losing too much blood, Landon." I glance up to see if he can hear me. "He needs a hospital."

Landon's full attention is on the road ahead of us.

"Dalton." I attempt to wake him. "Dalton, please wake up."

Dalton stirs, but his eyes remain closed.

"Which way am I going?" Landon shouts.

The vehicle makes a sharp left a few seconds later, jolting Dalton and I toward the door before we shift back into place once again. The vehicle resumes a high rate of speed.

I hear a deafening crash, jerking my attention out the back window, just in time to see one of the vehicles go off the road, flip over and come to a rest on its side. I pray hard that it's Alistair or his brother Antonio. As I continue to watch, I notice there are three vehicles left and I really want to know who they belong to.

Landon steps on the gas pedal pushing the vehicle to its max limit as we fly over the roadway which is a lot smoother than the field.

I glance down at Dalton whose eyes slowly open.

Breathing a sigh of relief I run my hand over his face. "You're alive?" I'm happy to see his baby blues.

"What's happening?" He coughs then winces in pain.

"Stay put." He's lying on his side with his head in my lap as I press the cloth to his wound, trying to hold him still. He attempts to sit up, but I push him back down. "Don't move," I instruct, as I restrain him which is easier than it should be. He's weak from having lost so much blood. "You've been shot."

He attempts to roll over.

"Don't," I repeat.

He settles down pulling his legs up and bending them on the seat to get more comfortable. "Where are we going?" He sputters and coughs. "Who's driving?"

The SUV shifts hard right and I grab a hold of Dalton, preventing him from rolling on the floor. He groans. "Landon?" I shout, not really sure if I'm answering Dalton or yelling at Landon to be careful.

"We're almost there," Landon calls from the front seat.

I look back at Dalton who has shut his eyes again. "Dalton." I rub his arm careful not to jerk him around too much to avoid further aggravating his wound. "Dalton, wake up."

His eyes blink open then shut once again.

"Hurry, Landon," I yell.

We shift hard left again.

"What are you doing?" I cry out.

"Trying to lose the car behind us," he barks.

I look over my shoulder and out the back window to see only one vehicle following close behind us. Turning back around, I lower my eyes and behold the gun lying on the floor by my feet.

I prop Dalton against the seat, as I reach for the gun. "Do we know who they are?" I question, while weighing the cold metal in my hands.

"They're not mine," Landon says, as he pulls the steering wheel to the right and I tumble sideways into Dalton who is being tossed around like a rag doll.

"Slow down, Landon." I adjust myself back into my seat.

"I can't. Their gaining on us," he snaps.

"Let them." I cock the gun. "Let them come up beside us."

"Are you crazy?" he shouts.

"Do as she says," Dalton yells.

Landon slows the SUV.

I wait until the other vehicle is right at the back of our car before I roll down the window, lean out, aim the gun and pull the trigger. The vehicle veers off to the right before losing control and slamming into a wooden fence rendering it disabled.

I press the button to roll the window up and put the safety back on the gun before returning it to the floor at my feet.

Dalton's eyes are wide open, his head leaning against the headrest as he stares at me.

Landon slows the SUV to a more manageable speed and keeps glancing in the rear-view mirror at me.

I remain quiet wondering what they're all staring at.

"Where'd you learn to do that?" Landon asks, his voice in awe.

"Jr. State Rifle Champion," Dalton answers for me.

I turn to him in shock before I remember he's an FBI agent, or was, or whatever. I peer back at Landon. "That, and my dad's a cop, remember?" I throw in for good measure.

"Right," he says with a small grin, the first I've seen him smile since being here.

"How are you doing?" I pick up the abandoned cloth on the seat and motion for him to lean forward. It's awkward, but I manage to get a look at his wound from behind. It's still bleeding—badly.

"I'll be fine." He leans back against the seat.

"How long, Landon?" I ask.

"We're here." Landon skids off the road onto a long driveway.

I watch out the front windshield as we travel up a never-ending road that appears to lead nowhere. There are empty fields on both sides of us and a forest area up ahead. I squint my eyes trying to figure out where we are to no avail.

I rest back against my seat and check Dalton who is extremely pale and is obviously in pain. I extend him a look of sympathy.

"We'll be there in a minute," Landon attempts to reassure us as he pulls up to a heavy-duty steel gate with barbed wire across the top. The entire set up looks intimidating.

Landon pulls up next to a box, rolls down his window, and presses what I'm assuming is a code and the big heavy gates begin to open.

"We have company," he blurts out.

I snap my head around to peer out the back windshield. A vehicle is coming in our direction, tailing us at a high rate of speed along the stretch. I scramble to pull the gun off the floor, releasing the safety as I push the button to roll down the window.

Landon floors the gas pedal which lurches the car forward and causes me to bounce back into my seat.

Dalton groans. He's slumped over with his head lolling on his chest. I shove him against the headrest for support. I turn to look out the side window for the vehicle in pursuit, but the gates have closed behind us, leaving no visual.

Landon tears up the roadway leading to several buildings. He comes to a halt in front of one, shoves the gear shift in park and jumps out.

Dalton's door abruptly swings open and two men who are dressed in scrubs reach for him. I slap their hands away as I grab Dalton and hold him to my chest. My door springs open and Landon reaches for me.

"Don't touch him," I yell at the man latching onto Dalton.

"Let them help him, Lexi," Landon insists.

Reluctantly, I let Dalton go.

One man leans in the doorway and pulls Dalton out. The

other grabs his shoulder, while the first man grabs his legs. They haul him onto a waiting gurney. *Who are these people? This is not a hospital, but it's sure starting to resemble one.*

Landon helps me out of the car, slipping an arm around my waist and leading me to the building. I hear tires squealing on asphalt and spin around to see the vehicle that was chasing us at breakneck speeds is now coming to an abrupt halt behind us. I stiffen, waiting anxiously to see who will emerge from the vehicle.

"It's Leroy," Landon says.

I sag in relief as I watch the passenger door open and Leroy materialize out of the vehicle. Taking him by surprise, I run straight at him throwing my arms around his neck, nearly knocking him over.

"I thought we lost you." I'm probably making a fool out of myself, but I don't care. I pull back and look him over from head to toe. "Are you okay?"

He gives me a wry smile. "Yes. I'm fine." He looks me over. "Are you good?"

"Yeah. I'm good. You know me." I grab him again for another hug. "I have nine lives."

We share a giggle—yes, Leroy giggles too. Strange coming from this hulk of a man, but I love the sound. "I'm glad to see you're all right, Leroy." Landon's voice projects from behind me, and Leroy lets go of me. It's strained. "Casualties?"

"None, Sir," Leroy responds.

Landon puts a damper on our reunion.

"What happens now?" I ask.

"First," Landon begins. "We get inside." He grabs my hand, towing me toward the building, Leroy on our heels.

The building is a nondescript concrete structure resembling a factory from back home.

Landon pulls the handle on a solid steel door that protests under movement, emitting a screech as he swings it open. He motions for me to enter ahead of him, so I step over the threshold. We enter a long hallway where I wait for Landon or Leroy to guide the way.

Leroy strides past me and I fall into step behind him.

Landon puts a hand on the small of my back guiding me along.

Walking along the corridor, we pass several closed doors before finally coming upon one that's open. We enter.

In the center of the room, lying unconscious on a gurney, is Dalton. I run immediately to his side and take hold of his hand, while scanning the tubes coming out of his arm and nose.

"How is he?" I ask, no one in particular. Since all three people are wearing scrubs, I've no idea who the doctor is. Or, whether any of them hold a medical degree at all. When my question goes unanswered, I get annoyed. "How is he?" I repeat a little louder hoping someone will answer.

The three people, two men and a woman, stop what they are doing and look up at me. After a moment of silent staring, two go back to whatever they were doing before we entered. One of the men comes over to stand in front of Landon and me. He begins talking to Landon as though I haven't said a word, aggravating me even more. If I weren't so concerned about Dalton, I would give this man a piece of my mind.

"All injuries are minor. Although the bullet missed the major artery, it's lodged in his scapula." He pauses to take in our blank stares. "Shoulder blade." He continues, pointing to his shoulder for effect. "So, we're going to have to pull it out, but it's a minor procedure."

"Pulling a bullet out of someone doesn't sound that minor to me." I look at Dalton's handsome face. His eyes are closed making it seem as if he is sleeping, but I know better. I brush some of his blond hair back from his forehead. "Stay with me."

A hand on my shoulder brings reality into focus. I glance at Landon to see the compassionate expression on his face and know that is why I fell for him in the first place. That look is like a window into his soul and what a beautiful soul it is.

"Let's allow the doctors to do their jobs," The expression on my face must give him pause. "We can get cleaned up." He glances down at his attire, or lack thereof, before his eyes meet mine again.

"You go ahead. I'm going stay with..." Landon's tone cuts me off.

"Lexi. You have to let them work," he snaps, anger crossing his features, before they soften when he pauses to pinch his nose between his thumb and forefinger.

"Lexi?" Leroy calls out from the doorway. "You'll be in the way."

I glare at him, eyes narrowed, eyebrows knitting together ready to tell him off. The sympathetic expression on his face stops me in my tracks. He's not trying to be difficult. He's not even trying to tell me what to do. He's concerned—for me and Dalton. It's because of this concern that I turn to Dalton, grab a hold of his hand and squeeze. I lean down, bringing my mouth to his ear and whisper. "Come back to me."

Releasing his hand, I turn around and walk toward the door with Landon following behind. Once we step back into the hallway, I spin on Landon.

"Now what?"

CHAPTER 26

*A*fter Landon deposits me in a room that resembles an army bunker more than guest quarters, he tells me to clean up and rest. But, who can rest? I'm still somewhere in Italy, we've been in a gun fight, a car chase and had to run for our lives. How can he expect me to rest?

I scan the room for the hundredth time, taking in the bunk beds along two walls, footlockers at the end of each set and a doorway leading to the bathroom on the back wall. This place reminds me of the army barracks my cousin lived in when he underwent basic training. I got the chance to visit him and was given a tour. The whole place has the same set up, igniting my curiosity in speculating why this place exists?

Reaching the end of my patience, I hop off the bed, and rush over to the door, intending to go check on Dalton. Once I grip the door handle giving it a twist, to my horror, it's locked. I try again, confused by my discovery, truly believing I'm wrong, only to realize it won't turn. Frustrated, I begin pulling and pushing the door as my foot gets in on the action. I kick, scream and pound on the steel structure unable to budge it.

What the hell?

I'm trapped.

When my knuckles feel sore, and my foot throbs from kicking the hard steel, I quit and make my way back to the bed. I plop down on it's hard surface and expel a huge sigh.

I really am trapped.

I try to keep calm but panic is rising within. My heart pounds in my chest as if it's attempting to escape.

How am I going to get out of here?

Why am I locked in here to begin with?

Just as a panic attack threatens to overtake me, I hear the door click. I scramble off the bed and run straight for the steel structure. It springs open just as I reach it.

Landon stands on the other side fully dressed and obviously showered.

I run straight into his arms colliding with him so hard I knock the wind out of him and he expels a puff of air.

"What's the matter?" he asks.

With my arms tight around his neck I squeeze him hard. He stands still for a minute before his hands wrap around my waist and he hugs me back.

After a moment's pause he loosens his grip, holds me at arm's length and gives me the once-over from head to toe. "Are you okay?" He narrows his eyes for a closer inspection. "What's wrong?"

"I thought..." I stumble over my words. "I thought...

well, since the door was locked..." My words are cut off immediately.

"The door was locked?" Landon steps around me to inspect the door.

I can see when realization dawns on him, it's truly like a light bulb going off over his head. "Damn it," he bellows as he reaches up to run his hand through his hair then pinching the bridge of his nose between his forefinger and thumb. "Lexi, I'm so sorry," he exclaims. "The doors automatically lock." He turns to face me, dropping his hand, pain etched in his features. "I would never lock you in on purpose. Please, forgive me."

My heart slows as my nerves return to normal. It was a mistake. Just a mistake. I hold Landon's gaze for a moment to make certain he's being truthful and it seems as if he is. Although, that doesn't stop the scared feelings I have from creeping through my mind.

"You didn't get a chance to clean up." Landon looks me over once more. "Would you like a moment to freshen up?"

"No," I blurt out quickly. "I just want to check on Dalton."

Landon remains silent for a moment, the expression on his face hard to decipher. *Is he mad? Jealous?* Before I can figure it out, his mask slips back into place.

"Come. I'll take you to him." He extends his hand.

I slip mine into his finding comfort in the warmth that envelopes me the minute we touch. No matter the circumstance, even surrounded by danger, my body still reacts the same way it always does when in the presence of this man.

Landon tugs me and leads us down the hallway.

I practically have to run to keep up with his long strides and now I'm certain he's jealous. It's clear from the way he looked at me and the way he's ignoring me now.

Finally, we round the corner and head into the first open door. There lying on the same gurney in the center of the room is Dalton, fully awake and attempting to sit up.

"Get your hands off me," he shouts at the doctor who is attempting to hold him down.

I drop Landon's hand and rush to Dalton's side.

"Don't try to get up." I grab Dalton's hand.

"Lexi." He relaxes back on the gurney. "You're okay?" He half states, half questions.

"I'm fine. It's you I'm worried about." I push the hair out of his eyes with my free hand.

"I'm fine, but this…" He jerks his thumb at the doctor, "guy won't let me up."

"You were shot. You need to rest."

Landon joins us, standing next to me.

As their eyes meet an enormous amount of tension fills the space between them, the silence in the room—stifling. Dalton drops my hand as they continue their staring contest. It's apparent to me that I'll have to put an end to this—whatever this is. I turn to Landon.

"What happens now?"

"You two go home." His tone is cold and clinical. I don't recognize this man at all. He turns around and walks to the door.

"I'll be right back," I give Dalton's arm a pat then rush after Landon.

Once in the hallway, I race down the hall coming up behind him. "Landon?"

He continues on his way without even a glance back.

"Landon?" I yell.

He stops in his tracks and spins around.

"What, Lexi?" he sneers.

"Where are you going?"

"Back to work." He turns to start walking again.

"Don't do that. Talk to me."

He turns to face me and three strides later he comes to a halt right in front of me. "What do you want from me?" His voice is full of hurt and pain.

"I want you to tell me what's going on?"

"I'm making arrangements to get you two out of here." He waves one hand at the doorway. "That's what's going on."

"And, what about you?"

"What about me?" He plays dumb.

"Are you coming back with us?"

"No."

I'm crushed. Devastated. *How could he not be coming home?* We got him out of there—freed and yet, he won't come home with us. The panic I felt earlier returns in full force as I clutch at my chest to stop the pain from the hammering of my heart.

Straightening out to my full height in complete defiance I square my shoulders and level him with a glare. "I'm not leaving here without you."

"Yes, you are. You have no other choice." He spins around and continues down the hallway once again.

Astonished, I stand frozen in place. My heart tells me to run after him, except my brain can't seem to make my feet move. Instead, I stare at the empty hallway far too long.

"He's not mad at you," Leroy's voice infiltrates from behind.

"Yes, he is." I don't bother to look at him because my gaze can't seem to budge from the empty hallway.

"No, he's mad at your friend in there, and…" he pauses waiting for my attention, so I spin around to face him. "He's mad that things didn't go according to his plan."

"And what plan was that, Leroy?" I ask knowing I probably won't get a straight answer, or an answer at all.

He glares at me, disappointment spreading across his face. I realize how unkind I'm being to him, but he deserves it. He, and the rest of these people have kept me in the dark long enough. Now they seem to be directing their anger at the wrong person. Dalton isn't to blame for any of this. He's not to blame for my being here. It's quite the opposite, in fact. I'm to blame for him being shot.

Quickly, my thoughts turn back to where they belong —Dalton.

I head back into the room where he is lying on a gurney with a bullet wound to his shoulder. Marching over to his side, I grab his hand once more giving him my best apologetic face.

"Lexi. Will you stop?" he admonishes. "This isn't your fault."

"Yes, it is." I lower my head, unable to make eye contact with him. "First, I drag you here. Then, I leave you out there for them to shoot you up. Of course, it's my fault."

My eyes remain downcast to the floor in my refusal to look him in the eye.

He sighs. Loudly. "Lexi?" he projects. "Look at me. Please."

I hesitate, trying to control the tears that are stinging my eyes before I peek up at him.

"This isn't your fault, darling." He reaches out brushing away a few stray tears that have slipped down my cheek. "I'm fine. They fixed me up and I'm almost brand new." He smiles.

I feel worse. How can he be so sweet when he's lying here with a bullet wound to his shoulder, and no appreciation from anyone around here?

"Hey." He reaches over, placing a finger under my chin, tilting my head up to gaze into my eyes. "I'm fine." He smiles wider.

I give him a small smile back.

"Now." He lets go of my chin, bracing his hands on the gurney. "Let's get out of here." He pulls himself up to a sitting position, legs dangling off the gurney.

"Dalton, lay back down. You're hurt." I reach my hands out to push him back down, but he pushes them away. "You shouldn't be getting up. You need to rest."

"No. What I need to do is find out what is going on around here." He jumps down off the gurney, groaning slightly.

"See, you're in no shape to be moving around." I actually stomp my foot with my hands on my hips—not one of my finer moments.

"Relax, it's not that bad." He reaches behind himself,

scooping up a shirt off the gurney and tries to put it on. He struggles to slip his arms into the shirt, while I refuse to help him out of stubbornness.

Leroy, of all people, steps up beside him and gives him a hand, all the while glaring at me.

I glare right back.

"Thanks," Dalton mumbles.

"You're welcome," Leroy says, then walks to the door.

Dalton follows him.

I stand, frustrated as I watch them retreat from the room. I glance over to one of the doctors who is also staring at the doorway. He glances at me, shrugs his shoulders, then goes back to doing whatever it is he does around here.

I rush out the door to try and catch up to them.

They are just rounding the corner at the end of the hall, so I step up my pace to a jog not wanting to lose them. This place is enormous and too easy to get lost.

"Wait," I call out.

Dalton halts his steps and spins around.

Leroy, who is a few paces ahead does the same.

Both stand watching me as I approach.

"You two should go back to the infirmary." Leroy points back down the hallway.

"No," I speak for both Dalton and myself. "We're coming with you."

Leroy tilts his head back, lets out a sigh, and glares up at the ceiling.

After a few short seconds, his head drops forward and

his gaze darts between Dalton and me. "He's not going to like this," he mumbles, mostly to himself.

"I. Don't. Care," I snarl.

"Fine." He turns on his heels and stomps down the hallway.

Dalton and I start after him, completely amazed at his transformation to a three-year-old before our eyes. I swear the only thing he's missing is the foot stomp and the statement, 'it's not fair.'

I struggle not to giggle, because seriously, the way he's acting is hilarious. I've never seen a grown man pout, and right now that is exactly what he is doing.

He turns into an open doorway and we follow cautiously a few steps behind.

The room is a security office or some sort of command center. Three walls are lined with monitors. Each wall has about fifty different monitors with fifty scenes being displayed.

There are ten men in the room, each sitting at their own desks, and each monitoring their own control panels and equipment. All are wearing headsets and intently watching the screens.

I survey the room startled at the surveillance happening in front of me. Although, I really shouldn't be surprised after witnessing Landon's surveillance room. This room is much larger with a lot more equipment.

Dalton immediately moves further into the room, inspecting all the screens in admiration. He scrutinizes each one before he pans around the room at the men working behind their desks. It's as if he can't believe his own eyes as he vacillates between the men at work and the displays on the wall. Suddenly, he stomps over to the wall on the left, coming to a stop in front of a scene that catches his eye. He runs his hand through his hair as he glares at the screen.

I walk up and stand next to him to look at what grabbed his attention. There in front of us is the cottage we've been sharing for the past two weeks. The view is of the kitchen area where the scanner still sits on the table and I can see the window where I stood vigil. If my calculations are correct, the camera is sitting right above the desk Dalton sat behind on a daily basis. There are also five men ransacking all of our stuff while Alistair and his brother Antonio stand by.

The screen beside it shows a view of the hallway leading to the front door. There are two more each displaying Dalton's room and mine.

I gasp.

"How did I not know this," Dalton says, mostly to himself.

"Yes. How?" Landon's voice breaks through my shock as I glance over my shoulder to see him walking towards us. He stops right next to me. "I thought you were an FBI agent. I thought you were well-trained. How is it that we had cameras on you the whole time and you knew nothing?" Landon's voice reveals the anger he possess as he snaps at Dalton.

Dalton closes his eyes, and his brows furrow, berating himself, but Landon's not finished yet.

"How could you not anticipate Alistair's reach? Did you

not think he would know that you were barely a mile from his home?" Landon shoots daggers at Dalton, waiting for an answer that doesn't come. "And, not only did you put yourself at risk, but you drag her along with you?" Landon points at me as he throws his accusation at Dalton.

"He didn't drag me along." I spin to face Landon ready to give him a piece of my mind. "As a matter of fact, I dragged him into this. It was my idea. I booked the trip. I made it happen. He just came along to make certain I wasn't going to get myself killed in the process." I take the two steps that closes the gap between us and start jabbing my finger into his chest. "We came here to help you. To bring you home, but I guess we were wasting our time. Weren't we?" I drop my eyes to the floor, trying to gather my thoughts. "I just wanted to bring you home safely."

"Lexi?"

Glancing up, our eyes met and I can see the concern flash in Landon's eyes, or is it heartache? It's hard to tell.

"What Landon? What would you have me do? Leave you here?"

"I want you to go home." He runs his fingers through his hair, breaking eye contact with me for a moment. "I want you safe and sound."

Tears sting my eyes as I stare at Landon. He's dismissing me—again. I'm trying to understand why he doesn't want my help, why he doesn't want me.

"I'm not leaving without you." I lean toward him.

He lets out a sigh as he directs his next statement to Dalton. "You will be leaving. Arrangements have been made for both of you to return to the States." Landon leans closer to Dalton. "I entrust that you *will* see her safely home." The anger toward Dalton rolls off him in waves as he glares at him with disdain.

"What the hell is the matter with you?" I ask.

Landon's glare is suddenly aimed at me as our eyes lock. We remain that way for a few moments before he says the five words that shatter my heart.

"I don't want you here."

He spins on his heels and strides out of the room.

Silence swirls around me, bordering on nothingness.

Everyone in the entire room has stopped what they are doing to look at me. The tears that were threatening to fall have now rolled down my cheeks, but I swipe them away embarrassed that I still care. Anger is building in me as I glance around the room planning my escape.

Leroy steps forward wearing the utmost compassionate expression on his face.

"Don't," I simply say to him.

His expression lasts another second before it's wiped clean and Leroy, the businessman emerges. "The chopper is waiting," he announces, his gaze travelling from mine to Dalton's.

I should be surprised. In fact, under any other circumstances I would be, but right now, I'm not. "Of course it is," I mutter as I walk out the door.

I want to go home.

CHAPTER 27

I wake with a start, my body shaking and my mind cluttered. It takes me a moment to process what is happening, but once I do I realize Dalton is shaking my shoulder to wake me. I take a second to gather myself and emerge from my drowsiness.

"Where are we?" I peer around the cabin for any sign.

"We've just landed. They're taxiing the plane to the gate so we can leave," he says so casually, as if it's normal behavior to be on a private jet returning from a fun-filled vacation, but that is not what happened here. And, my mind replays it over and over on a constant loop.

"There's a car waiting for us." Dalton turns, walking toward the front of the jet.

I take a moment to stretch and look around at what should be an exciting sight. A large cabin with the most comfortable seats, explains why I dozed off once we were in the air. There is a bathroom and even a bedroom with a huge bed. I would have enjoyed sleeping in the bed, but couldn't find it in myself to venture in there. Everything is top of the line, but I expect nothing less from Landon. It would be thrilling to be on this jet going somewhere exciting or romantic, but sadly that is not the case. We are headed home—without Landon—and as usual, my life is in ruins. My heart aches knowing I left him there with those people even though I know it was his wish.

I didn't truly leave of my own free will. I was kicked out, tossed to the curb... Told I wasn't wanted which finally broke me. I could see my efforts were not appreciated. And so, while licking my wounds, I got on Landon's helicopter to begin the long journey home.

Gathering myself and my wits, I stand up and move to the exit. It's like I'm dragging myself along with no thought, no mind. That's it. I'm mindless. Or, completely exhausted. I haven't decided which one yet.

Dalton, on the other hand, is doing pretty good considering he was shot in the shoulder. I ought to be paying more attention to him. I should be making certain he is taken care of, instead it's the other way around as usual. But, I'm shattered. Lost. I can't even begin to think of what I will do now.

Exiting the plane, I drag my butt down the awaiting staircase truly not noting whether the crew of the jet are there or not. I know I will wonder later if it's like the movies where the crew greets you upon entering and exiting the plane and I'll wish I had noticed. But, right now, my mind is frazzled and I just want to go home.

As I step to the ground, safely back on US soil, I trudge forward to the waiting vehicle, my eyes glued to the cement below my feet. I do notice Dalton's cowboy boots clicking along in front of me and wonder how he found the strength to make this trip. He was shot. Actually shot. And, here he is making sure I get home safely. It's not right, but out of my hands.

As we reach the vehicle, I glance up for the first time. Standing right before my tired eyes is the person I need most in the world but don't deserve to have greeting me. I run the last few steps right into Haley's arms as the floodgates open leaving me sobbing like a child.

Haley, the ever-loving best friend, holds me tight chanting in my ear that everything will be 'all right.' She rubs my back, doing all the things that I don't deserve after the way I treated her.

"I'm sorry," I mumble into her shoulder.

"Hush, now. Let's get you home." Haley leads me to the backseat of the vehicle.

Dalton is already seated, talking on his phone, laptop on his lap while he types. I frown wondering what he is doing, fully aware he has no job to concern himself with. Which reminds me that he and I will be having a conversation about all the things I learned on this trip.

For now, I lean against Haley closing my eyes in an attempt to block everything out and draw some of her strength to help me heal.

I barely remember arriving at my house or being guided to my bed, but I wake sometime later and glance around the room. It seems such a long time ago since I was here plotting and planning to save Landon. Little did I know, he didn't want rescuing.

Sitting up, I notice the room is empty, no sign of Dalton and absolutely nothing to let me to know that Haley was not a figment of my imagination coming off that jet. As I swing my legs over the side of the bed, I hear hushed voices coming from somewhere in the house. Looking down at myself, I realize I'm still in the clothes offered to me on Landon's jet.

Getting out of bed, I cross the room to my closet and walk in to find something else to put on.

With an outfit in hand, I march into the bathroom for a much needed shower. Throwing my clothes on the vanity, I strip out of the dirty ones I'm wearing, and spin the taps on to start the shower. Setting the faucet to its maximum potential for "hot," I wait the few seconds required before I'm shrouded by steam. Stepping in, I revel in the exquisite feeling of the water running over me. Feels like it's washing all my problems down the drain. It's so cleansing. I would cry, but I'm pretty certain my tear ducts are empty. Instead, I stand under the spray, letting it return me to my some-what normal existence—for the time I'm in the shower, anyway.

Freshly cleaned and clothed, I decide it's time to face my company. I leave my bedroom and make my way to the living room.

Haley is sitting on the couch with her feet tucked up under her and holding a book in her hands.

Dalton is propped on the armchair typing furiously on his laptop.

As I enter the room, Haley throws her book down on the couch and extends her legs so her feet touch the floor.

Dalton peers up from his laptop staring at me as I walk into the room and take a seat next to Haley on the couch.

I feel like an animal at the zoo with the way these two are studying me waiting for me to break down any moment. I can't blame them for that really, I have been a tad unpredictable. But, no more. My days of breaking down are behind me. Now, it's time to get my life back. Enough is enough. I've played this game far too long.

"Are you doing okay?" Haley asks.

"Yes," I sigh.

"So, what now?"

"Now." I glaze at her then Dalton who is glaring at me. "Nothing."

"What do you mean… nothing?"

"It's over, Haley. Look at poor Dalton." I wave my hand in his direction. "He was shot. Actually shot. He's lucky to be alive," I huff.

"Hey. It wasn't even close." He acts offended by my statement.

I roll my eyes knowing how close it actually was. Then, an overwhelming sadness seeps through me for having dragged him into all of this and he ends up getting hurt. *How can I ever make this up to him? Why is he even here?* If I were him, I would have dumped my butt off and been gone.

"You don't have to hang around, Dalton. I'm good now that we're home." Much of his life has been wrapped up in my problems.

"I don't feel comfortable leaving you alone, yet." He goes

back to typing furiously, completely ignoring my state-ment and Haley and me for that matter.

"So…," Haley says, as she turns fully on the couch to face me.

"I'm so sorry, Haley," I blurt out as tears sting my eyes.

"Yeah, sure. We'll talk about that later." Her eyes flicker to Dalton and back. She reaches out, grabs my hand and gives it a squeeze. "Tell me, what happened?"

"A lot. I don't even know where to begin." I turn on the couch bringing my legs up and sitting cross-legged in order to face her.

I give her the entire run down, starting with landing in Italy, our surveillance of Alistair's property, getting caught, the chase, the shootout, our escape and finally—being dismissed and sent home by Landon. To Haley's credit she sits quietly as I relay the entire ordeal.

"Wow, Lexi," Haley states. "Just wow."

She turns her attention to Dalton.

"Are you sure you're going to be okay?"

"Yes, I'll be fine." He looks up from his laptop and joins the conversation.

"What have you been doing?" I point to the computer sitting on his lap.

"Finding out everything I can about Antonio Marzano. My ex-boss," Dalton replies.

"Why?"

"It's apparent there are some things that need to see the light of day. Starting with who he really is." Dalton shrugs as he goes back to typing.

I glance at Haley who shrugs her shoulder too.

"So, what now?" Haley asks me.

"Now. I work to reclaim my life." I drape my arm along the back of the couch granting Haley my undivided attention. "I want to make things right with us, Haley. I'm so sorry."

"I know you are." She smiles as she pats my hand. "We'll get through this." She winks at me. "We always do."

"You're too good to me." A tear rolls down my cheek. I guess my tear ducts aren't dry after all.

"I know, but trust me when I say." She gets a strange look on her face as her voice projects a lot deeper than normal. "Someday, and that day may never come, I will call upon you to do a service for me."

Haley's voice cracks as she breaks character and we both burst out laughing. A good deep laugh that has tears rushing to my eyes and my body bending at the waist.

"*The Godfather* is no laughing matter, girls." Dalton chides us with a straight face while pointing his finger in our direction.

Both Haley and I struggle to stop laughing as we stare at him.

After a few seconds we all burst into laughter. It feels good to laugh. It feels like it's been forever since I've laughed, or had a good time, for that matter. That stops now. I think I've had enough adventure to last a lifetime. I want to go back to a simple life where my biggest worry is what's for dinner. Where I don't have to worry about being killed, or having someone I love killed. Yeah, I think it's time to come back to the real world.

"Seriously though... what are you going to do now?" Haley asks.

Our laughter stops.

"I don't know. Go back to work. Move." I shake my head as I answer. "I really don't know."

"Well, you don't have to figure it out today." Haley gives me a reassuring smile.

"Dalton?" I look over at him.

He peeks up over the top of his computer.

"What are you going to do now?" I'm actually curious as to what a former FBI agent does once they leave the Bureau.

He sits up straight, closing the lid on the laptop. "Well, first things first. I'm going to take care of the Marzano brothers."

"How many are there?" Haley pipes up.

"Three. I think," he says. "But, I'm having trouble locating the third one." He puts the laptop on the table beside him and stands up to stretch out his limbs. "Do you mind if I?" He points towards the bathroom.

"You don't have to ask." I watch as he walks out of the room, then turn my attention back to Haley.

She sits back, a big smile—a weird smile—across her face as if she's in on some secret I'm not privy to.

"What?"

"Nothing," she smiles wider.

"That smile is not nothing."

"You like him," she giggles as she whispers her statement.

"No," I refute. "Well, yes. Not like that."

"It's okay if you do, Lexi." She giggles again, and it's annoying.

"I don't. Not in that way," I whisper back.

"Okay, okay. I get it," she says with that infuriating smile still plastered across her face. "But..." She turns her torso to glance down the hallway before looking back to me. "He is cute." She winks.

I begin laughing.

"Yeah, he is." I hear footsteps coming and turn in time to see Dalton walking back into the room.

He looks at us funny as he strolls across the room and resumes his seat in the chair across from us. His eyebrows furrow.

"What's so funny?" He's suspicious of our behavior.

"Nothing," I reply immediately, not giving Haley a chance to embarrass me as I rein in my laughter. "How long are you planning to stay?"

"Until I know you're safe," he replies without hesitation.

"I'm safe now. I'm home. Everything is good, no need for you to worry," I try to reassure him, but he doesn't appear reassured—at all.

"Lexi, we're talking about some of the biggest criminals in the world. I'm not leaving you alone until they are dealt with. End of story." He picks up his laptop, opens the lid and resumes whatever it is he does.

I look at Haley for guidance, but the look on her face tells me she's not going to be any help.

"Well, I'm getting hungry." I get up from the couch and walk into the kitchen.

"I'll help." Haley also rises from her seat and follows me.

For the next five days, I'm held captive in my home by Dalton, who has become my uninvited guest and protector. He never leaves, but he's usually preoccupied by his laptop or phone. I'm not exactly certain what he's up to, but I'm getting quite tired of sitting around the house.

Haley has been here daily, checking up on me, bringing me essentials that apparently I can't go out and get on my own. Even though I don't deserve her friendship, I'm so glad she's here. Without her love and support, I don't know what I would have done. Not sit around here that's for sure.

According to Dalton, the authorities are closing in on the Marzano brothers and arrests will be made within a couple of days. I seriously don't think I have anything to be concerned about when it comes to the brother's. I barely know them or their criminal activities. There's no reason for them to seek me out, but Dalton doesn't see it that way, so he remains a fixture in my house 'until the entire mess is dealt with'. His words, not mine.

I, on the other hand, spend my days catching up on my charity work which has taken a backseat since all this began. But now, it's time to get back to the things I was working on and guide my life in a more positive direction. The way it's gone for the past several months is not what I hoped for.

There's been no word or sign of Landon. Not that I expect anything different. Okay, yes, I wish he would contact me, but only to let me know he is safe—alive even. The truth is, I miss him terribly and wish I knew what is happening. My concern grows each day there is no word from him or anyone on his team. However, I suppress those feelings, wishing them away. My life with Landon is not meant to be. I must accept that and move on. That's what my head says, but I wish someone would explain it to my heart.

Finally, on the fifth day we get word that the brothers Marzano were arrested and held without bond in Italy. The list of charges are numerous and they are all facing life in prison.

a week has passed since the arrests, and my life slowly returns to normal. At least, normal as life can be after everything that's happened. I resume my charity work and have even been to a few interviews for job prospects. Now, I just have to decide what it is I want to do. I can re-enter the legal profession. However, due to the circumstances of the past few months, I'm not convinced it's the path I want follow.

Haley tried to convince me to work for her, but I knew working for my best friend was not something I wanted. Her company is great, but fashion is not my area of expertise. She offered me the position of in-house council. However, she already has an attorney, and the arrangement is not something I'm interested in. I believe in earning a position rather than having it handed to me.

Dalton, on the other hand, left my house on the fifth day, and I haven't heard from him since. Although, I miss him terribly considering we spent more than a month together on a daily basis, I knew he needed time to re-build his life. Even as he left my house, he was unclear about what he was planning to do now that he no longer worked for the FBI. I tried to convince him to go back and explain his position, but he was reluctant.

Still no word from Landon either, not that I expected to hear from him. He is back in the US and safe as far as I've been informed. Curiously, I received a bouquet of blue and white roses with no card accompanying them. I believe they came from him because of the meaning behind the flowers. Of course, being the crazy person I am, I googled their meaning. Blue roses stand for attaining the impossi-ble, whereas the white roses stand for innocence and purity. Even after everything that has happened, Landon still believes I'm something I'm not.

It's probably for the best that he's been reluctant to contact me because I know I'm not strong enough to resist him—yet.

My life has fallen into a fairly boring routine of working on my charities in the morning and job hunting in the afternoon. I have dinner with Haley in the evenings, which I'm positive, is her way of keeping an eye on me without me knowing that's what she's doing. Except, I know her better than that, and chalk it up to her concern about my well-being.

We finally had the talk that was long overdue. One night, we sat and hashed out everything I hid from her—all my omissions of information and why I felt the need to keep her in the dark.

In the end, we shed a lot of tears, burdens weighing us

down. We cleared the air of everything, including why she felt the need to keep her lifestyle choice a secret. We also came to the conclusion that I was never meant for that lifestyle as shown by my refusal to mind my own business and not meddle in Landon's.

I'm no submissive—that much is evident.

Tonight will be my first night truly alone since arriving back from Italy. I've convinced Haley to go out with her new beau whom I've insisted on meeting. And, apparently, that would happen the very next night. Tonight, however, I'm looking forward to a quiet, relaxing night doing a whole lot of nothing.

As I settle down on the couch with a book at the ready and a cup of freshly made tea beside me on the end table, a loud knock at the front door disturbs my peace. I get up from the couch to find out who is disturbing the solitude I've so perfectly planned.

Swinging the front door open, I encounter a man with black, shoulder-length hair. He has deep-set dark eyes, and eyebrows pinched together. He glares at me. He's wearing a long, black trench coat. Left unbuttoned, I get a glimpse of his suit, which is also dark in color. A white-collared, buttoned-up shirt with a blue tie. A finely dressed man for sure, but his glare lets me know this is not a social visit. This man is not to be trusted, making me regret my decision to open the door.

As we stand staring at each other, it becomes apparent he isn't going to say anything, so I begin.

"Can I help you?" I'm annoyed by the stranger standing on my porch.

He narrows his eyes further but remains quiet. He's calculating something—what, I have no idea. But, he's definitely trying to figure something out.

"What can I do for you?" I huff, my voice sounding as aggravated as I feel.

Still, the man stands on my porch staring at me without uttering a word.

Irritated to the point of hostility, I start to swing the door shut intent on ignoring the man who doesn't seem to have anything to say. A foot unexpectedly protrudes between the door and the frame, preventing the door from closing. Anger fills me as I rip the door open again, only to discover the man is closer than I feel comfortable with.

He reaches out, grabbing me by the throat and squeezing. I struggle as the man backs me up until he's inside the house. He closes the door with his foot and pins me to the wall with his hand still around my throat. He puts enough pressure to scare me, but not enough to choke me.

I struggle against his hold, while he levels me with a glare.

"Do you know who I am?" He tilts his head to one side.

"No." I struggle harder.

"Stop fighting me," he demands. I don't listen and keep trying to pry his hand off my throat. "I'm not going to hurt you."

I don't believe a word he says as I continue to fight.

"Stop," he bellows making me shudder.

In that moment, I realize his identity which he must sense by my expression.

"You know, don't you?" he asks again, as he loosens his hand slightly.

"Armand," I whisper and cough at the same time.

"So, my reputation precedes me?" he asks, but I'm not sure he wants an answer.

"What are you doing here?"

"Are you kidding me?" His face appears shocked by my question. "I'm here to find out what… woman," he spits the word 'woman' with such disgust, "could possibly take my family down."

Anger is rolling off of him in waves and I'm terrified, more terrified than when I was going up against his brother. Armand is ten times scarier than Alistair. As I remain pressed against the wall my mind is working over-time trying to find a way out of this situation. It's not looking good.

"I didn't take down your family." I shake my head back and forth.

"Yes. Yes you did." His hand tightens around my neck.

I grab a hold of his wrist, struggling to break free as my air supply is being cut off.

"Our business was fine until I heard your name. Since you came along, my brother has become obsessed." His hand squeezes harder. "You were taking away what was his. Did you think you could do that? Did you think there wouldn't be consequences?" he shouts, sounding like the crazy man he is.

I struggle harder against his hold, but there is no budging him.

"You can't bring down someone's business without paying the consequences," he growls.

"I didn't do anything. I don't know what you're talking about," I cry out.

"Yes, you do. You came to Italy trying to shut down our business. But, guess what? We're too big for you, little girl. You messed with the wrong family this time." His hand squeezes tighter.

I can feel myself slip from consciousness. My air is being cut off as I panic. I struggle as hard as I can, but he is so much stronger than me. I'm in the hands of a madman who thinks I've ruined his life. There's no getting out of this.

His eyes burn in rage, nostrils flaring, and his breathing is labored as he stares straight into my eyes. I've never seen a psychopath, but I believe I'm staring at one now. He brings his free hand up to my cheek and brushes away the tears that are running down my face. The gesture is odd as he squeezes a bit harder on my throat. I can feel my eyes bulging, my throat gasping for any bit of air it can get, but it's no use. This is how I'll die. At the hands of madman.

I hear the front door burst open, hitting the wall hard as a blurry figure steps over the threshold. I can't turn my head, but move my eyes in that direction attempting to see. I can't quite make out the person.

I hear shouting as my eyes close and everything around me ceases to exist. My world goes black.

CHAPTER 29

*M*y head is sore, my body aches as my brain struggles to figure out where I am and why I have the biggest headache I've ever had. I roll over onto my side, but immediately roll onto my back. My entire body feels like one big bruise. *What the hell happened to me?*

I try to open one eye, but the light hurts my brain, so I squeeze it shut tight. I think about the last thing I remember and it all comes rushing back. Armand. Him choking me, the crazed look in his eye. *Am I dead?* I don't think so. I wouldn't hurt this much if I were dead—*would I?*

I remember the front door slamming against the wall.

I lift my hand, bringing it up to my neck touching it experimentally to assess the damage. It's raw to the touch feeling like a rug or rope burn. I touch my face tracing along tracks of dried tears on my cheek, and what I'm sure is another bruise, but can't remember how it got there.

I open one eye. "Ouch," I whisper against the bright light, but continue to strain against it. My other eye opens and my eyes adjust to the light. My head pounds as if I were drinking all night and now have a hangover. The biggest hangover I've ever experienced.

I try to sit up and the room spins.

"Woo, don't try to get up." My head pounds from a familiar voice I struggle to recall.

Am I in danger? Is the nightmare not over?

I struggle harder to get up as two large hands push me back down, pinning me in place.

"Stay. Don't try to get up," the voice says softly, but the hands hold tighter. "You're safe. I promise."

My eyes focus on the person speaking and I realize it's Leroy.

"What happened?" My voice is hoarse almost non-existent.

"Rest." He lets out a sigh of what sounds like relief. "It's been a long night and you need your rest." He runs his hand over my hair tenderly.

"Tell me, Leroy." I need to know what occurred.

Leroy rubs his fingers across his forehead, back and forth, over and over.

"Please," I beg him. "What happened to Armand?"

His head snaps up as he does a double take.

"What did you say?" His tone registering his shock.

"Armand. Where is he? What happened to him?" My voice leaking out as a whisper on account of my raw, sore throat.

"Is that who did this?" he asks me with narrowed eyes.

"Yes." I wonder why he doesn't know. "Wasn't it you

who stopped him?" Again, I try to sit up, but Leroy pushes my shoulder back down.

"No, it wasn't me, Lexi." He gets up from the bed and walks across the room, picking up a cell phone from the dresser top. He jabs the screen a few times, then puts the phone to his ear.

I scan my surroundings puzzled, nothing is familiar. I roll my head to look at the other side of the room, and still don't recognize anything.

"It was Armand," Leroy says into the phone.

He pulls the phone from his ear, jabs the screen once again to end the call. He turns around and places it back on the dresser as he grips the dresser top with both hands. His back rises and falls as he takes deep breaths.

"Leroy?" I call out, but get no response and try again. "Leroy, where are we?"

Leroy turns around, eyes full of sympathy. He takes a few strides to reach the bed and sits down beside me.

"Tell me, Leroy. Where are we?" I'm becoming increasingly annoyed the longer he stalls.

"We're in a safe house."

"A safe house?" I sit up against the headboard.

"Yes. It's belongs to Mr. Miller." He leans to the side, grabs a glass of water and a bottle of pills. He hands me the glass, takes the cap off the bottle and shakes two out handing them over to me. "Aspirin," he claims as he drops them into my open hand. "For your headache."

I arch my brow at him.

"You took a pretty hard hit. Or, so I'm told." He touches the side of my face which is tender and sore to the touch.

"Was it…?" I blink away the tears that are stinging my eyes. "Was it, Landon?" I say his name with hesitation.

"No, it was Agent Johnson who saved you." He gets up, walks across the room, opens a door and steps over the threshold disappearing from sight.

I pop the pills into my mouth and take a big gulp of water before Leroy heads back into the room with two towels in his hands. He sits back beside me on the bed, approaching my face with one of the towels.

I flinch from his touch.

He looks at me sadly and sighs.

"Sorry," I mumble, embarrassed.

"It's okay." He reaches out again. "I'm just going to clean you up a little." He presses the towel to the side of my face gently.

"How bad is it?" I wonder aloud because it feels like I've been hit by a Mack truck.

"It's going to be black-and-blue for a while, but nothing permanent." He gives me a small smile.

I nod my head, letting him know I understand.

"What happened, Leroy? How did I end up here? And, where is Dalton?" I ask anxiously, pushing his hand away.

"We're not exactly sure." He leans back, placing the towel on the nightstand. "*He* got a call from Dalton asking if *he* had a secure location for you," he explains, and I immediately know the 'he' is Landon.

"So it was Dalton who saved me?"

Leroy nods his head in the affirmative.

I think back to the moment my front door swung open. Between not being able to breathe, and tears blurring my vision, I couldn't tell who had come through the door. Still can't piece it together, even with the knowledge it was Dalton. I do remember being hit across the face and flung to the floor like a rag doll, though. That memory is one I wish I could forget.

"Where is Dalton now?" I wonder, obviously out loud.

"We don't know. He called asking for a safe place to put you. I picked you up and brought you here." He waves his hand displaying the room.

"Where is here? You said this is a safe house. Safe from what, exactly?" My curiosity is through the roof. *Why does Landon have a safe house?*

Leroy sighs heavily as he stands up, walks to the dresser and leans against it, facing me with his arms crossed and one foot over the other. He's shutting down on me and I know he won't give me the answers I so desperately want.

I huff. Flinging the blanket off, I swing my legs over the side of the bed. Planting my feet firmly on the ground, I attempt to stand, but drop back down as the room spins and nausea takes hold. Placing my head in my hands, I try to stop the onslaught of emotions coursing through me.

"It would do you well to remain where you are. You probably have a concussion. You shouldn't try to get up." Leroy's voice is so clinical, resembling nothing of the man I woke to.

"You can't keep me here." I release my hands from my head and glower at him.

The look he gives me tells me loud and clear he can, in fact, keep me here. I'm too weak to fight him even if I wanted to, which I don't so I give in. This is Leroy and even though, at the moment, he's trying to show his strength and power, I know better. Leroy is kind, considerate, and very much a gentleman. If he thinks I should stay here for my own safety, I should take his advice. However, I'm sick and tired of being treated like glass. I thought when ushered into the helicopter to leave Italy this whole nightmare would be over.

Guess I was wrong—very wrong.

I sit back against the headboard and glare at him.

He remains still as a statue watching me.

"So, how long am I supposed to stay here?" I ask folding my arms over my chest, mimicking Leroy's pose.

"Till it's safe for you to return home," he states so casually, as if this happens all the time. And, maybe in his world it does, but in my world...

"So, what? We're just supposed to sit here and wait?" The anger flows through me at a rapid pace.

"Yes."

"Leroy? What went wrong? I thought they arrested the brothers?"

"We thought they did too. That was what our Intelligence told us. Apparently, we were wrong." He picks the phone up off the dresser and begins swiping his fingers across the screen.

"So, is Armand the only one not in custody?" I wonder what happened to the other brothers.

"We believe so," he answers without so much as a glance in my direction.

"What time is it?"

"Eleven."

"It's eleven at night." I try to remember the time just before Armand showed up to my door, I believe it was early afternoon. That's a long time to be unconscious.

"It's morning," he replies, again not looking my way.

"Morning?" I shout out in surprise. "Why am I not in a hospital? How could you keep me here—unconscious, no less? What is the matter with you people?" As my rant continues, I stand up. My nausea forgotten, and the aspirin doing its job taking care of my headache.

Leroy finally glances up from the phone in his hand to glare at me.

"This is crazy. I'm leaving." I take a few steps toward the door, which I'm hoping is the way out.

Evidently it is because Leroy moves in front of it and shakes his head.

"I can't let you do that." He stops me.

"Get out of my way, Leroy," I say through clenched teeth as my hands form tight fists at my side.

"I'm sorry, Lexi. I can't do that. I have my orders."

"Either let me out, Leroy, or I'll be forced to move you."

My hands squeeze into fists so tight I think my nails will break the skin. The small trace of a smirk displayed on Leroy's face angers me more. Without forethought or hesitation, I raise my foot and kick him in the shin.

He doubles over, grabbing his leg and hopping around in pain as he yells at me.

"Damn it, Lexi," he screams out as he rubs his shin where my foot connected.

I take a defensive stance, while thinking of my next move. I could hit him again and send him to the ground, but as he peeks up at me I see the pain in his eyes. Pain, not from me kicking his shin, but rather, pained that I would do such a thing to him. As guilt washes over me, I stand down and reach for him.

"I'm sorry, Leroy." I grab his arm to try and help him stand.

He rubs his shin quickly, drops his leg to the floor and stands up to his full height. His face contorts displaying the intimidating glare I've seen him use at the club.

He takes a step forward and I take a step back.

For a tense moment, I think he's going to hit me, but then his face softens and he gives me a sympathetic pass.

"This is for your own good. We're only trying to protect you."

"But, from what, Leroy? You still haven't told me what is going on? Why are the brothers free?" The questions tumble from my lips.

"I would tell you if I knew. I'm not exactly sure what's going on or who is free. There's nothing to tell at this point," he replies, but his expression lets me know he's not being completely truthful.

I concede, for now.

"Where's the restroom?"

Leroy points to a door across the room, which leaves one other that I assume is a closet. I cross the room, go inside and lean against the door, taking a deep breath. I stay there for a moment catching my breath and allowing my mind time to process everything.

Releasing a deep breath of air I walk over to the sink and turn the taps on, adjusting the temperature to a comfortable setting. Looking around the vanity, I spot face cloths rolled up and stacked neatly in the corner. Hand towels hang on either side of the sink on towel holders. I run my hands under the flow of water and I glance up peering into the mirror.

Shock courses through me at the sight of my face. My left cheek is black-and-blue with a small cut in the center. My left eye is black and swollen, how have I not noticed this? As I run my hand over the area it's sore to the touch. I look like I've been beaten, which I guess I was.

Around my neck are ugly, red hand-prints turning into blue, black and yellowish bruises. Hesitantly, I reach up to run my fingers across the marks. They too, are tender to the touch. I'm a wreck. No wonder they all think I need protecting. Apparently I do.

Grabbing a face cloth from the side of the vanity, I run it under the water getting it good and wet. Dragging the cloth across my face, slowly and lightly, I can feel the extent of the damage that monster caused. I turn off the taps, reach for a hand towel and pat my face, careful not to press too hard.

I move back to the door and crack it open to peek out.

"Leroy?"

Leroy comes to the door, standing back a few steps.

"Do I have a change of clothes here?" I'm hoping someone thought that far ahead.

"Hang on a sec," Leroy mumbles as he walks out of view.

A few seconds later he returns holding a duffle bag out to me.

I take it and shut the door. I walk over to the toilet, close the lid and place the duffle bag on top and unzip it. Inside the bag are clothes, along with a smaller bag sitting on the very top. I reach in, pull the smaller bag out and place it on the vanity before snatching out some of the clothes. Relieved, I pull out a couple of T-shirts and two pairs of jeans. At the bottom of the bag are a couple of pairs of socks, a few pairs of underpants and a bra, all of which are all neatly packed. As I take the bra out, I wonder who put the bag together as embarrassment overtakes me, imaging Leroy rummaging through my dressers looking for my intimates.

I walk over to the shower, spin the taps on before stripping out of my clothes. I step into the shower stall and immediately bask in the warmth of the water as it cascades down my sore and tired bones. Plunging my head under the spray, I close my eyes and let the flow envelope me like a comforting blanket. All stress slides off of me and down the drain. There's nothing like a hot shower to heal the soul.

After a few more minutes of letting the worry slough off my body, I begin my cleansing routine. I have to hand it to the people who run this place because anything I could ever want or need is available for the taking. Leroy said this is a safe house, but now I'm wondering what that means? *A safe house for whom? And, what do they need saving from?* These questions join a long mental list of questions to ask Leroy when I return to the bedroom. The hard part is getting him to give me answers.

After shampooing my hair and washing my body, I

close the taps turning off my oasis. I regret it immediately when I pull back the shower curtain and get a wave of cool air surrounding me. Stepping out of the shower, I grab a big, fluffy towel and wrap it tightly around me. Then, I reach for another to wrap around my head and contain my hair.

My mind keeps replaying the same thought over and over, 'How did I end up here?' It's like a broken record that keeps skipping. It feels like I'm reaching the point of insanity.

A few teardrops fall from my eyes as I swipe my hand across the mirror to clear the steam away and glance at myself. I look different—older than my twenty-five years. That thought has my mind skidding to a halt. Twenty-five. When did that happen? Even worse—in two weeks I'll be a year older. Sigh.

Once my hair dried sufficiently, I gather it in a ponytail, courtesy of the hair-ties I find in the smaller bag. Rummaging, I also come across a brush, comb, toothbrush, toothpaste, deodorant, and a bottle of my perfume. I leave the bathroom and step back inside the bedroom.

Leroy is sitting at a small table in the corner that accommodates two. He has a phone against his ear and a laptop in front of him on the table.

I drop the duffle bag on the bed before walking over to the table. I pull the chair across from him out and take a seat. I prop my elbows on the table, clasp my fingers together and rest my chin on the pedestal of my hands.

I stare at Leroy while he speaks.

"I understand." He nods his head as if the person on the

other end can see him. "No. Everything is under control."
More head nods before he pulls the phone away from his
ear, presses a button and throws it on the table. His fingers
immediately start typing on the computer as his gaze is
drawn to the screen. "Feeling better?" he asks, without a
glance in my direction.

"Yes."

The silence grows between us as Leroy does whatever it
is he is doing and I sit staring at him.

"Why does Landon have a safe house?" I blurt out.

Leroy peeks at me over the laptop screen, but he doesn't
speak.

"Leroy?"

"You know I can't answer that. So, please don't ask me."
He lowers his eyes back to the screen in front of him.

Dropping my hands to the table with a bang. I sigh. *Am
I supposed to sit here, doing nothing? Until who knows when?*

"What is going on out there? When will we be able to
leave?"

Leroy glares at me over the screen again.

"I can't just sit here," I argue as I slam my hands on the
table in frustration.

My thoughts turn to my plans tonight, which angers me
even more when I realize my dinner with Haley and her
boyfriend will not happen. "I need to use the phone."

Leroy, who is still glaring at me, sighs heavily as his
features become softer.

"What, Leroy? Is using the phone out of the question
too?"

"Yes," he practically whispers.

"Why?"

"Lexi, we're in a safe house. No one can know where it is. That's kind of the whole point."

"Oh." I hadn't thought about that. "But, you're using the phone?" I point at his phone.

"It's a burner. Untraceable." He shrugs his shoulders as his attention returns to the screen.

"Can I use that one, then?"

Leroy peeks around the screen and glances at the phone. His gaze meets mine and I can tell he is considering it.

"I just need to call Haley. We were supposed to have dinner tonight. She'll worry,"

"Fine." He expels a gust of air through his lips. "But, make it short, please."

"I will." I reach out and pick up the phone. I quickly turn it on and dial Haley's number before he can change his mind. "I promise." I give him a smile as I put the phone to my ear, get up from the chair and cross the room to the bed. It rings a couple of times while I sit on the edge of the mattress.

I'm disappointed as the phone rings for the sixth time, then clicks. I'm prepared to leave a message on her voice mail when I hear a male voice answer.

"Hello."

I pull the phone away from my ear to look at the screen to check the number I dialed. Seeing it's the right one, I put the phone back to my ear and hear the male voice speak again.

"Hello."

It strikes me this could be Haley's boyfriend.

"Hi. Is Haley there?" I ask.

"I bet you were expecting her to answer." The voice is unnerving. There is something completely off.

"Yes. I was. You must be the boyfriend."

"Wrong again." The voice sounds amused, but I'm not. I stand up straight and glance across the room at Leroy.

He takes his attention away from the computer screen to look at me.

"Who is this?" I ask, panic evident in my tone.

"Oh, I think you know," he toys with me.

My whole body begins trembling.

"Where is Haley?"

"Where are you?" he counters.

Leroy dashes across the room, ripping the cellphone from my hand and placing it to his ear.

"Leroy." I holler.

He puts his finger up to quiet me as he listens further.

"Who is this?" he asks.

I move to stand next to him so I can hear both sides of the conversation.

"Leroy. So good to hear your voice, but I believe I was conversing with Mrs. Shaw."

"Now you're talking to me. Where is Ms. Rose?"

"Now, now, Leroy. Do you really think you're in the position to demand answers?" The man laughs and I realize its Armand.

"Just answer the question."

Leroy walks across the room to the table and his

computer. I follow along, standing beside him as he sits back on the chair. I lean closer to him in order to hear.

"How about we make a little trade." Armand laughs once again. "Haley for Lexi."

"Not going to happen, and if you hurt..." Leroy is cut off.

"Do not threaten me, Leroy. I promise it won't work out well for you," Armand warns.

"What do you want?"

"Revenge." Armand's words echo through my head.

Haley and I are paying the price for a war that has existed between these men for who knows how long. Rage pours through me as I grab the phone out of Leroy's hand, put it to my ear and walk a few steps away.

"You listen to me, pal..." I begin. "If you so much as touch a hair on..." I'm cut off by a clicking sound. "Hello." I'm met with complete silence. "Hello." I try once more and nothing.

"Great." I lower the phone from my ear and hear a loud sigh from behind me. I can't turn around because I know I messed up and probably cost Haley her life. I feel my shoulders shaking, my heart pounding as a scream escapes my lips and I fall to my knees.

"Oh, God. Oh, God." Those words keep rolling off my tongue. "I've killed her. I've killed her."

Two strong arms wrap around my midsection, lift me off the floor ease me gently onto the bed.

Looking up at Leroy, who's blurry due to the tears filling my eyes.

"She's going to die because of me."

"Lexi, stop," Leroy demands.

I close my eyes and take a few deep breaths before peeking back up at him.

"Are you sure this is Ms. Rose's number?" He holds the phone in front of my face.

I work to control the tremble rippling through me as I brush my hands across my eyes, clearing the tears away and glance at the phone.

"Yes, that's her number," I cry out as the trembling begins all over again.

"Stay with me."

Leroy lets me go and walks over to the table to take his seat. He types into his computer pausing long enough to hit speed dial on the phone, putting it on speaker and laying it on the table. It rings twice before someone answers.

I get up and move to stand next to him as a voice comes out of the speaker on the phone.

"What's up?" A familiar male voice answers.

"I need someone to find Haley Rose," Leroy snaps as he goes back to typing on the laptop.

"Haley Rose. Got it. Give me twenty minutes," the male voice, who I now recognized as one of the bartenders at Landon's club, replies.

"You've got, ten," Leroy hisses.

The line goes dead.

Leroy reaches over and presses the "end" button and gets back to his laptop.

My attention is completely consumed by the lifeless phone as I pray for it to ring and deliver us good news.

The only sound in the room is Leroy's fingers hitting the keyboard as the minutes tick by, or perhaps it is mere seconds, I'm not really certain in my distraught state.

"You should sit down," Leroy suggests without glancing up, his entire attention consumed by the computer screen.

I look down at his screen. "What are you doing?"

"I'm signing into our network in order to locate Ms. Rose's phone." His fingers fly across the keyboard.

Suddenly, a map appears that has a whole lot of red dots popping up across the screen. As I watch, the map begins filling with red dots and I become more confused.

"What are they?" I point at one of the red dots.

"They're all cell phones."

I stare at Leroy, stunned.

"Whose?"

"People in our network," Leroy replies nonchalantly.

I scan the screen to see what must be hundreds of dots.

"What network?" I ask, shocked at the sight in front of me.

"Lexi, please. You know I can't answer your questions. So, please stop asking." He glances up at me for a moment before going back to his work.

I go back to glaring at the phone, willing it to ring.

Finally, after a long wait, it plays a song. Much to my chagrin, Leroy reaches over, picks up the phone and brings it to his ear, essentially shutting me out of the conversation.

"Tell me what you've found." He glares at the screen.

Leroy clicks the mouse on the screen which zooms in on the map, eventually giving us a street view of the dot

Leroy clicked on. In front of my very eyes, Haley's house comes into view.

I gasp. Stepping backwards, I bump into the wall.

"What is it?" Leroy turns around in his chair to look at me.

"It's Haley's house."

"That's good news." Leroy relays this information to the person on the phone.

I'm shocked as I look at the screen displaying the front of her home, wondering how this can be good news.

"I'll be watching." He listens for a moment longer. "Hey, be careful," Leroy hits the screen of the phone and places it on the table.

"What's happening? What's going on?" I step over and stand behind Leroy once more.

"Go have a seat. Try and relax. We'll find her." He avoids looking at me.

I move around the table, grab the chair and drag it beside Leroy's. I sit down and watch the screen.

"Not exactly what I had in mind," he mumbles, as his gaze remains focused on the screen.

"Too bad."

We sit in silence, both concentrating on the screen in front of us. All is quiet and only the odd car drives by, which is not surprising for the neighborhood. Haley's street has always been quiet.

The wait is killing me. First, I have no idea what we're waiting for. Second, if anything happens to Haley I'll never forgive myself.

My leg bounces up and down as I bring my hand to my

lips and bite my nails. I can feel my frustration level rise as we wait. Waiting has to be the worst thing we are ever required to do. It feels like it's been an hour. Yet, only ten minutes have passed.

My body is coiled tightly ready to blow like a volcano as my attention remains glued to the tiny screen in front of us. Three cars pull up to the curb on the street in front of Haley's house. Two men emerge from each car and descend on the property, surrounding the house.

"Who are they?" I nervously ask Leroy.

"They're ours."

I lean in closer to get the best view I can. Another car pulls up and three men jump out, joining the other six. Each man head in a different direction, strategically spreading out around the property. Two walk to the front door and the others go around the side of the house and are hidden from view.

I watch, eyes glued to the monitor as the two men at the front door open it and head inside.

"What are they doing?" I blurt out.

"They're checking the house." He shrugs his shoulder.

"What if she's in there? She'll be terrified."

"They wouldn't have gone in if she was home." He gestures at the house with his hand. "They know what they're doing."

A few tense minutes later, the men walk back out the front door and the phone on the table rings. Leroy scoops it up quickly, he presses "talk" on the screen and brings it to his ear.

"Report," he commands.

I watch him closely for any sign that will tell me what is happening.

"Are you sure?" His gaze remains on the screen. "You've checked the basement, attic?"

Leroy must make on hell of a poker player, the man gives nothing away as I glare at him wishing he would offer a morsel—anything.

Leroy sighs heavily as I return my attention to the monitor where I'm able to spot one of the men with a phone to his ear, and conclude he is the one speaking to Leroy.

All of a sudden, one of the men from the rear of the house comes running out to the front gesturing at the two men to follow him.

The man with the phone to his ear drops his arm and begins jogging toward the other man. When he reaches him, they all jog around the side of the house disappearing from sight.

Leroy, who holds the phone to his ear, watches the screen intently.

"What is going on?" I'm quickly losing my patience.

"I don't know." Leroy leans closer to the screen. "It looks like they've found something."

"Is it Haley?" I too lean in for a closer look. "Have they found her?"

"I don't think so." His voice sounds agitated.

We wait in silence as time ticks by, both staring at the screen, not moving, probably not even blinking. In the dead silence of the room, I hear what sounds like a muffled explosion and turn my attention to the phone at Leroy's ear. His eyes widen in shock for a second before he reins them back in and they return to normal.

"Was that a gun shot?" I plant my face in front of the screen, scrutinizing the entire property.

"I don't know." Leroy is busy scanning the screen too.

"Oh my God, Leroy." I jump out of my seat and begin pacing the floor. "What is happening? Where the hell is Haley?"

Leroy pulls the phone away from his ear as the sound of more muffled gunshots come through the speaker. Stopping me in my tracks, I stare at the phone. It sounds like a war movie as shots ring out every few seconds. Peering over at the screen, there is nothing to see but I can't help but stare.

Three more cars pull up near the house, coming to a halt in the middle of the street. Several men emerge from their vehicles fully-armed looking like a tactical unit. They quickly sweep through the front yard, splitting up, where half go around the left side the house, and the second half run around the right side. They are dressed in black from head to toe. All are wearing bulletproof vests and helmets. Each one carrying a different type of firearm.

The last man to emerge from the vehicles is moving slower than everyone else as he makes his way to the front of the yard. He stands, head moving back and forth between the left side of the house and the right. He is dressed like the other men and has a gun in one hand and a phone to his ear with the other. I'd know this man anywhere.

Dalton walks over to the front door and peeks inside.

Leroy ends his call quickly and dials another number.

On the display in front of us I see Dalton pull the phone away from his ear and look at the screen before he presses it, placing the phone back to his ear.

Again, I hear muffled shots coming through the speaker.

"Leroy," Dalton blurts out.

"They have him pinned down out back," Leroy says.

Dalton peeks over to the left side of the house.

"Go, now," Leroy commands.

Dalton takes off running around the left side of the house before disappearing from sight.

"I thought you didn't know anything," I retort.

Leroy's gaze snaps back to mine before returning to the scene in front of us. It's apparent he has no intention of answering me.

On the screen I see men starting to appear from the side of the house. The first two make their way to the front lawn, then several more come around to join them.

Leroy breathes a sigh of relief.

"What is it? What's happening?" I plop back down into my chair.

"It's over," he declares, but does not elaborate.

On the screen, I notice more men coming around to the front yard.

Local police are beginning to arrive on scene as several lights are flashing red and I hear sirens blaring from the phone.

Dalton appears at the left side of the house and makes

his way to the front yard where the rest of the men have gathered. He places his phone back to his ear.

"What is he saying?" I ask anxiously.

Leroy waves me off, making my angry.

Why is he refusing to tell me anything?

"I heard." He shakes his head. "Yeah, it's all taken care of." Leroy's gaze remains on the screen.

A few of the local police have joined the group on the front lawn. I watch as the men gesture wildly making it evident they are informing the police as to what took place. Nice that they get informed.

"Where is Haley, Leroy?"

"Lexi," Leroy huffs as he turns to face me. "We're not sure."

"Oh, God," I return my attention back to the screen.

A car comes to a screeching halt behind the last police car on the street. I'd know that driving anywhere. Relief floods through me as Haley whips open the driver's door and steps out of her vehicle obviously stunned at the sight in front of her. She slams the door shut which garners the attention of the group of men standing in her front yard.

They all turn to gaze at her, but it's Dalton who grabs my attention as he turns to look at her. A huge smile spreads across his face as he speaks into the phone.

"I can see that." Leroy smiles for the first time since I woke this morning.

"What's he saying?"

"He said she's pissed," Leroy explains with a slight chuckle.

"Well, of course she's pissed. Look at what she's come home to." I wave my hand at the scene in front of us.

"What happened to Armand?" I glance at Leroy.

"He's dead," he deadpans as his gaze returns to the screen.

I stare at him for a moment, letting this new information sink in.

"So it's over?" I ask unsure. "Like, really over?"

Leroy turns to look at me. "I believe so." He ends the phone call with Dalton without a good-bye or anything. I watch the phone as he pulls up his call list and hits a number, placing the phone back to his ear.

"It's done," he states as he turns his gaze back to the computer. "Yes, Sir. Right away." He presses "end" on the phone as he reaches out, closes the browser on the computer and shuts it down. He stands from the chair and peers down at me.

"We're done here. You can return home." He walks around the back of my chair and heads to the bathroom.

I watch as he disappears, closing the bathroom door behind him. I get up and walk to the bed, grab my overnight bag, head over to the door, drop the bag to the floor and wait. I'm overly anxious to get out of here and want nothing more than to return home. I want to call Haley and make certain she is okay.

Leroy emerges from the bathroom and without a word or a glance at me he walks to the door, swings it open and steps out into the hall. I follow.

CHAPTER 30

I open the front door to my house and head inside. Everything feels strange. It's as if it's not my home anymore, like I don't belong here.

I continue through the house to my room, where I drop the duffle bag on my bed before heading back to the living room.

On the end table beside the couch sits my cell phone, which I scoop up quickly and dial Haley's number. After two rings she answers.

"Lexi? Where are you?" Haley asks, her tone laced with anxiety.

"Haley? Oh my God, Haley? I'm here. I'm all right. How are you?" I blurt out, quickly.

"I'm standing in my living room trying to find out why my house looks like a war zone." Haley's admission reveals her angered state, but it's so good to hear right now. "Jesus Christ, I came home to find every cop and FBI agent in town camped out on my front lawn," she sighs in exasperation.

"Where were you Haley?" I ask to satisfy the thousand questions revolving around my mind.

"I spent the night out and when I came home to get ready for our dinner tonight, I found a thousand cops here. What the hell is going on, Lexi? They won't tell me anything," she snaps.

I hear movement in the background—what I perceive as high heels clicking on the hardwood floor.

"Hey, I hope you're going to clean up this mess before you leave." Haley is shouting at someone.

"Now, Ms. Rose. Is that any way to talk to the people who saved your life?" I hear Dalton trying to pacify her or mock her, it's hard to tell without seeing his facial expressions.

"Dalton. Did they find it necessary to wreck my house in the process?"

"I hardly think they wrecked your house," He answers masking his amusement.

"Don't mock me, Dalton. I'm really pissed here."

"I'm sorry, Ms. Rose. It must be hard to come home to this." He trails off as I imagine him gesturing around the house.

"It is," Haley replies.

"Haley, can you let me talk to him, please," I ask.

Leroy glances up from my armchair where he has his laptop open on his lap, and phone sitting on the side table. He's pretty much made himself at home which wouldn't bother me as much if he offered any information. But he hasn't. So, he can just leave for all I care.

I hold him prisoner with a death glare while I wait for Dalton to come on the line. Leroy raises his brow at me before his attention returns to the laptop.

"Lexi?" Dalton finally speaks.

"It's me," I answer.

"Are you okay?" he asks, concerned.

"I'm good. A little sore, but I'll heal. What's happening there?"

"Everything here is good. Now."

I hear Haley shouting in the background. "Everything is not good. Look at my house."

There is a small pause before he and I burst out laughing. It's such a relief to laugh out loud. My emotions have been all over the map since I thought something happened to Haley. Now that I'm reassured everyone is fine and Armand is dead, I can relax once again.

Sinking into my couch, I can feel my body releasing all the tension that's been pent up inside me since we left Italy. I feel truly free for the first time since Haley dragged me inside Landon's club.

I sigh when I think about Landon and all the events that have happened since meeting him. What started as an attraction has ended. Honestly, I have no idea where we stand, or what can possibly happen now. The pull I felt toward him has dissipated, and I no longer feel the need to go to him or find out how he's doing. It's strange. I'm Numb, empty inside.

I glance over at Leroy who is still immersed in his work.

"Dalton? Is it true? Is Armand really dead?" I check for my own sanity.

Leroy peeks up from the laptop.

I arch my brows at him this time.

He goes back to ignoring me redirecting his attention to the screen.

"Yes. Armand is dead," Dalton acknowledges.

"So, I'm free…"

"Yes. It's over," he responds quickly.

"Thank God." I release a breath I didn't know I was holding onto.

"I'm going to give you back to Haley now."

"Dalton?" I say quickly.

"Yeah?" he asks.

"Thank you." A genuine smile emerges.

"You're welcome, Lexi."

I hear him hand over the phone to Haley.

"I wasn't kidding about cleaning up this mess," Haley retorts before coming back on the line. "Lexi? I'm on my way," she declares.

"No, Haley. It's okay. I think I'm going to have something to eat, then head to bed. I'll call you later when I get up."

"Okay. But, when you feel up to it, we are going to sit down and have a nice long talk," she threatens.

"I know, and we will. I'll talk to you soon," I reassure her. "And, Haley?"

"Yeah?"

"I love you."

"Love you too, sweetie. Get some rest," she says before the line goes dead.

I peek over at Leroy.

"Pizza is on the way," he says, while his attention remains on the screen in front of him.

I close my eyes trying to rein in the anger I feel erupting in me. *Why does he act as if I have no opinion?* He didn't even ask permission to order dinner or if he can stay here. I get up from the couch and go into the kitchen.

Once inside the safety of my kitchen, away from Leroy's prying eyes, I lean back against the counter tip my head back and stare at the ceiling. I take ten breaths trying to calm myself down.

Pushing away from the counter, I then move to the cupboard, open the door and take out two plates, setting them on the counter. I pull a couple of paper towels off the holder and place them on the plates. I move to the fridge and pull out two sodas. Picking up the plates with my free hand, I walk back into the living room.

As I'm placing the plates and sodas on the coffee table, Leroy peers at me, a smirk on his face.

"Don't even," I warn.

"Don't what?" He holds up his hand in a gesture of surrender.

"You know what." My tone is a tad harsher than I realized.

The doorbell rings, interrupting our conversation.

I stand up to my full height in readiness to answer the front door, but Leroy's withering look stops me in my tracks. He places the laptop on the floor beside the chair, stands up and walks away. I sit back on the couch and wait for dinner.

Leroy returns a few minutes later with a couple of boxes in his hand that he places on the table. Opening them all, he reaches for a plate, taking two slices of pizza, some wings from another box, a napkin and a soda. He walks over to the armchair sits down placing the soda on the table beside him and his plate on his lap.

He glances up at me. "Help yourself. I'm certain you must be hungry." He waves his hand at the boxes before he begins eating his meal.

I get up, grab a plate, place two slices of pizza on it and grab the other soda before heading back to the couch to sit down. The first bite of pizza is like heaven. I didn't realize how hungry I truly am until that first bite.

We eat in silence for a few minutes before the questions in my mind won't let me rest. As I take the last bite of my pizza, I glance over at Leroy who is almost done eating his meal. I put my plate on the table beside me and take a sip of my soda before addressing Leroy.

"Is it really over, Leroy?" I wipe my mouth with my napkin.

"I believe it is." Leroy leans forward in the chair and places his empty plate on the coffee table.

"So, what are you still doing here?"

"Tying up loose ends." He eases back in the chair.

"I'm a loose end?"

"Lexi, you never should have been left alone in the first place," he growls.

"But, we thought they were all arrested. We thought it was over."

"Well, some people shouldn't think. Had I known you were alone, I would have sent someone to stay with you," he sighs, closing his eyes and rubbing his temples.

"How long do you plan on staying?"

"As long as it takes to make certain you are really safe." He shrugs nonchalantly.

I gaze at him for a moment trying to figure him out. *Does he really care? Or is he under orders? And, where is Landon? How come he hasn't been here?* I haven't even heard from him at all. The flowers? I'm not even certain he sent them.

I reach my hand down the side of the couch behind the throw pillow and feel the cold metal snuggled right where I left it. I run my fingers across the handle before pulling my hand free.

Leroy picks up his laptop and goes back to work. I watch him for a few minutes before exhaustion gets the better of me. I stand from the couch, stretching my arms above my head and release a loud yawn.

"I'm going to bed. Are you staying the night?" I ask, unsure what his plans are.

"I'm not sure." He shrugs again without taking his eyes off the screen.

"Well, there's a spare bedroom down the hall, first door on the right. Not that you don't know that already. There are spare toothbrushes in the medicine cabinet. Help your-self to anything you need," I offer because no matter what I feel at this moment… No matter how angry I may be with Leroy or Landon, doesn't mean I've lost my manners.

I walk around the couch on my way to the hallway. "See you in the morning. Maybe." I walk down the hall.

"Goodnight, Lexi," Leroy calls out.

I stroll into my bedroom and over to my bed. I pick up the duffle bag I placed there earlier and throw it on the floor. Grabbing my pajamas off the chair in front of my vanity mirror, I change before sliding under the bed covers, and sinking my head into my pillow. As soon as my head hits the pillow my world goes black.

CHAPTER 31

*T*he early morning light shines brightly on my face as I roll over and open my eyes. I feel relaxed, calm and refreshed for the first time in months. My life is returning to normal of that I'm certain. I stretch my arms over my head as I wake.

Pushing the covers aside, I sit up and swing my legs over the side of the bed. Standing up, I cross the room, and head into my walk-in closet. Shedding my pajamas, I pull out some yoga pants and a T-shirt.

After I'm dressed, I enter the bathroom to brush my teeth and hair.

Once I'm decent, I leave the bedroom and head to the kitchen to start the day off right for a change—coffee. Gathering everything needed to take make a whole pot, I get to work. While it percolates I lean over the counter and pull open the dividers that separate the kitchen from the living room. I half expect to see Leroy still sitting in the armchair but the room is empty.

I leave the kitchen and creep back down the hallway stopping by the guest room door. It stands open and I peek inside. The room is empty.

I go back to the kitchen, grab a mug out of the cupboard and fill it with coffee. Walking over to the fridge, I swing open the door and reach for the cream, pouring a splash into my mug before placing the carton back on the shelf and closing the fridge door. I take a sip of coffee and marvel at the exquisite taste as it swishes around my mouth.

I leave the kitchen area and go back to the living room. As I enter the room, I stumble almost spilling my coffee at the sight before me.

"Have a seat Mrs. Shaw." Alistair, who is sitting in the same armchair Leroy occupied mere hours before, waves his hand towards my couch.

I stand, staring at Alistair, not moving or obeying his command. He becomes agitated, gets up from the chair and begins pacing in front of the living room window.

"What are you doing here?" My voice comes out a lot calmer than I feel.

"You know why I'm here." His pacing comes to a halt as he turns to face me, his eyes narrow, face contorted with malevolence.

"No. I don't," I answer, anger rising in my voice.

"He ruined my life," he explains, pacing once again. "He came into my world, turned it upside down and tore it apart." He stops, turns and stares out the window which overlooks my front yard. It's clear he is waiting for Landon. "Now." His voice has an edge to it as his eyes bore into mine. "It's my turn to ruin his life. Turn his world on its head." He takes two steps towards me before he pulls his hand out of his pocket, leveling it out in front of him and aiming a gun right at me. "Now, have a seat."

I walk around to the front of the couch and sit down.

"Why me?" I ask, truly wanting to know why he picked me over any number of people he could have chosen to get his revenge on Landon. Surely, a relative would be a better choice, not that I want anything to happen to his family.

"Because he loves you." Simply stated with a resigned shrug of his shoulder.

"That's not true," I growl before I realize I'm doing it.

"Oh, but it is, Sweetheart. He's so in love with you." He spits out the declaration like it's something sour in his month. "It's sickening. I know all about you, Alexandria. You come from a good family. Wonderful childhood. Parents who love you dearly. Yes, they divorced, but that didn't affect you like most kids in that situation. You married too young, but rectified that the minute you met our boy. Didn't you?" he sneers at me. It isn't really a question, more an affirmation as he continues. "Then you dug your claws into Landon and you've never looked back. You don't even feel the least bit humiliated being a whore. Do you?"

His accusation is a slap in the face. *How dare he?* I don't get a chance to argue as he continues his tirade.

"You moved right in messing up all my plans. You changed him," he asserts, waving the gun at me, "and not for the better I might add."

I grab the throw pillow next to me, holding it tightly in front of me as I stand from the couch, daring to approach an insane man so close.

"I didn't change anybody," I refute loud and clear.

"Oh, but you did. And now, he'll never be mine again," he hisses.

"Are you insane? He was never yours," I yell at him. I know—probably not the brightest idea I've had—further agitating someone aiming a gun at your head. But, enough is enough.

"You don't know what you're talking about," he sneers at me.

"Why don't you enlighten me?"

"Landon's been mine a long time. You should know that he lived with me for a year. He can never love you. He. Belongs. To. Me." He emphasizes each word, jabbing his finger into his chest.

His revelation blindsides me. *Landon lived with this guy? No way.*

"When?"

"When, what?"

"When did Landon supposedly live with you?"

"What does it matter?" he asks. "Besides, I'm the one asking questions here."

"I just want to know."

"Many years ago, but I always knew he would return to me," he explains.

My heart slams into my chest as I realize what Alistair is claiming.

"Have you totally lost it? You held him hostage for a year. And you think what… that he loves you? Is that what you think? You're even crazier than I thought." I take a step closer to him. "He never loved you," I declare in an eerily calm tone, hoping he'll confirm my suspicion of what happened to Landon during his missing year.

"Shut up." He sneers, waving the gun at me to emphasize his point.

"In all your research about me there's something important you forgot," I say with a wry smile.

"And, what would that be?" he asks, intrigued.

I take a step closer and lean into him so there is only two feet separating us. I whisper. "My father was a cop."

He stares blankly at me, apparently puzzled as to what I'm implying.

I drop the throw pillow to the floor, snap my hand into place, aim my gun and pull the trigger. In the split second it takes to achieve this, I witness the surprise in Alistair's eyes before the bullet strikes him in the middle of his forehead. His head snaps back and it's another second before his body collapses in a heap on my living room floor.

I stand with my gun at the ready and peer closely at the fallen body.

The front door swings open crashing loudly against the wall. I whip my head and gun in that direction.

Leroy steps out of the hallway into the living room. He glances at me then at Alistair.

I hear another set of footsteps coming into the room.

Landon appears at the entrance of the living room, his

sight drawn to the body that Leroy is leaning over. "Is he?" he asks Leroy.

"Dead, Sir."

I observe two fingers against Alistair's neck, confirmation as any that no pulse is a sure sign of death.

"Shit," Landon murmurs.

After a moment of silence, I lower my gun.

"It's over," I declare.

Both men look directly at me, but say nothing.

I look down at Alistair. "He's not going to bother us anymore."

There is so much I want to say, so many questions that need answers, but as I look at these two men in my living room, there is nothing I want to know from either of them. There is nothing either of them could ever say that would begin to make sense out of anything that's happened since I set foot inside that club.

I see the sadness in Landon's eyes, the pain that will always haunt him. I realize he will never let me in enough to help him deal with his anguish. Whatever happened has caused too much damage for him to trust me completely. My heart cracks as I realize what I must do and why.

Looking Landon straight in the eye, I speak.

"After this mess is cleaned up." I wave my hand in the direction of Alistair's body. "I never want to see you again." I state with calm and cool conviction, contradicting my inner turmoil.

Landon looks like I've slapped him—hard.

"Either of you," I finish with a glance at Leroy.

Leroy appears hurt by my dismissal.

I place the gun carefully on the coffee table, turn toward the hallway to my bedroom, and walk away, not even a glance back as I leave.

A few weeks ago, Landon walked out of my life and now with a heavy heart I'm walking out of his.

READERS

THANK YOU, KINDLY

Well that was quite the journey. Lexi had her work cut our for her in this one, but I think she came out on top. But, will our love birds meet again in the future? Grab a copy of the final installment, Freedom Book 3 today.

Freedom Book 3 - The Mystery of Landon Miller Series

If you are so inclined to leave a review I would be overjoyed to hear your thoughts. Good or bad. It helps me grow as writer and I appreciate the time people take to review.

R.M. Gauthier

ABOUT THE AUTHOR

Constantly writing, R.M. Gauthier is always trying to produce new material. With two series under her belt and two more on the way, she will continue to work hard in order to bring her readers more of what they love. In the meantime, you can find all her works at the follow links:

Website
www.rmgauthier.com

Join R.M Gauthier's Newsletter and receive two free stories!

http://eepurl.com/dhB5xs

Dreams really do come true...

Early one afternoon, while working alone, Millie encounters a magical book that insists on being read. Similar books continue to appear, transporting her to strange realms, from the Fabulous to the bizarre, where adventure and romance rule the day. From Wizards to Werewolves, Dragons to Santa Claus, this parade of enchanting creatures opens her eyes to the events taking place around her.

If you believe...

If interested you can find it here: OUAFT on Amazon

Charlotte Rose runs a Christmas Store in Christmas town with her father. For years, she has enjoyed the town and all it offers. Her hopes and dreams have always revolved around the town and store, until a certain man materializes and turns everything upside down.

Arriving in Christmas Town, on assignment, Jack refuses to fall under the magic of the Christmas theme, using his dislike of the holiday season to shield him from its spell.

Christmas Miracle Series on Amazon

ACKNOWLEDGMENTS

There are several people who help with the resources for this novel, the trailer and the advertisements. It is with a special thank you, and a shout out to each person who helped make this dream a reality.

To "Designed by Freepik," for my chapter heading designs.
You can find their work here: **Freepik**
Footage for my trailer:
Unripe Content footage available here: **Unripe Content**
Mitch Martinez footage available here: **Mitch Martinez**
Cinetrove footage available here: **Cinetrove**

Music for trailer:
Ross Bugden, find his music here: **Ross Bugden**